Lila Monroe

I MARRIED
~~THE BARTENDER~~
~~A MYTHICAL CREATURE~~
THE WRONG MAN

(c)2013

Printed in the United States of America
First Printing: April 2013
Pink Pen Publishing
ISBN-13 978-0-9855072-8-2

Printed in the United States of America

www.muddybayoupress.com

To my best friend Kelly—
Thank you for always being there for me...no matter what.

Vision

$\mathcal{Y}ou$ would think that after sixteen years the feelings of regret and longing would have disappeared. They would have at least dissipated, like a thick fog that slowly gets broken down into a light mist by the overpowering rays of the sun. My desire to see him only seemed to grow. The boy, that time could not erase, left me with a wide variety of feelings.

Rejection.

Hurt.

Pain.

Longing.

Desire.

These feelings have all been my constant companion through the past sixteen years of separation.

Why am I thinking about him now? Well, that's easy to answer. There is not really a day that goes by that something does not remind me of him. The smell of my coffee brewing in the morning, the way the wind caresses my hair when I walk outside, the sounds of babies crying as I lay them in their mothers' arms. But tonight it is easy to know what has triggered my thoughts of Marco.

My small group of friends gets together out about once a week. Tonight we're having cocktails at the Blue Crab Pub in downtown Kentson, Texas. It must be mellow eighties night in the bar; a song by Cutting Crew is playing over the bar's sound system. Garrison and Rhett are sitting together discussing some sporting event. Poppy and Dixie are talking about work. I am following the conversation but not closely enough to participate. I'm paying more attention to the attractive Brazilian bartender with the Italian name—Adriano.

His dark hair is cut short at the sides but longer on the top. The silky strands keep falling into his eyes as he moves around the bar. *Why doesn't he just cut it?* I imagine its silky feel as he tosses it back for the umpteenth time. What's strange is that even though I am not touching it, I know exactly what it would feel like sliding across the sensitive flesh of my palm. I remember the feeling of Marco's thick silken hair running through my fingers. He would lay his head in my lap at the beach and my hands would instinctively find their way into his hair. My fingers ache to know the feeling again.

I know this bartender is from Brazil because of his accent. I have been to Brazil many times as a child. The last was about sixteen years ago. I spent three months there living with my great grandmother, Noni. I was seventeen then and had met a boy there that I would have been willing to run away with if he would have asked. Adriano reminds me of that boy. He reminds me of Marco so much so— it is almost painful.

There is something about those copper eyes. After practicing medicine for years, I have yet to come across anyone besides Marco who had eyes that exact shape and color. Thinking about Marco

always makes me happy. The only sad thing about my time with him was saying goodbye. At the time he had broken my heart, but I have forgiven the brutal words he cruelly spoke when we parted. He was my first lover, my first love. He would always hold that special place in my heart.

All I know at this moment is I have an overwhelming urge to see him. I feel as if he is the key to a problem I am having.

First, I need to explain that my particular brand of problems comes in the form of visions. Yes, psychic visions. Right now there is one vision in particular that I am having a hard time deciphering.

My name is Biddy Elliot and I was born in the veil. An infant is born in the veil when there is a covering or membrane over the infant's face—covering their unusual eyes. Mine are an exotic blue grey with copper flecks surrounding the pupil. People often describe them as being catlike. I even have one patient who insists on calling me Doctor Cat Eyes.

Being born in the veil is rare and most commonly occurs in females who are born prematurely. I was born four weeks early and from what my mother describes it was a bloody scene that left my aunt's white shag carpeting with a horrific red stain.

Infants born this way are endowed with special abilities. Seeing the future through dreams, talking to ghosts, and healing are usually the talents credited to them. They are also thought of as being extremely lucky individuals.

I can do all three.

My visions range from common everyday déjà vous to predicting the death of a loved one. Typically, those are the scary dreams. Those are the most memorable because the dead visit me in those dreams. I have a strange dream life mostly because I have lucid dreams and have been able to interact with those who visit me at night. Sometimes I wake up knowing that I had a dream and not be able to remember any of it. Other dreams are prophetic and unforgettable.

My latest dream had me stumped. *The sound of a baby crying in the adjoining room pushes me to check in on what is wrong. I peer into the white bassinet lined with soft pink blankets. She looks up at me and immediately stops wailing. She has a few tendrils of curly brown hair falling over her plump face. The majority of which is filled with large blue eyes and chubby cheeks tinged with coral pink centers. I lift up the silver rattle lying next to her and shake it gently to soothe her. The rattle chimes lightly. The tinkling sound makes her smile and coo. She reaches for the rattle. I hand the delicate toy back to her and notice that the rattle's handle is molded in the shape of a large cat's body; the tail circling the stem of the rattle. The cat is predatory. Its muzzle is open ready to attack prey.* How unusual. I have never seen a rattle like it before and the cat is almost scary. It is a strange choice of adornment for such a small child's toy. The cat or the rattle must be the key to the meaning of the dream.

This dream definitely contains something prophetic. After all these years, I have learned which dreams mean something and which ones are just my mind rewinding the previous day's activities. I do not have any control over the visions and I am not warned about every single life event. If I concentrate and open myself up to my abilities, I have the visions more frequently. I am

not always open.

When I was a teenager, I did practice divinations. My great grandmother taught me. She was born with special abilities like me. I really did not enjoy using the cards or stones my grandmother gave me to predict people's futures. It was mentally draining and my experience was that most people did what they wanted anyway … so why bother?

The most amazing of my abilities is probably my ability to heal. No one besides my great grandmother knew that I could do this. She taught me how and told me never to tell anyone. She said that when I was grown if I wanted to practice the healing arts I had to find a way to do it without drawing unwanted attention since I live in a world that was not accepting of such magic. It was easy for her to live the life of a healer in her small rural village, but when growing up in a modern city, it was just not an acceptable past time for a young girl.

That explains my current occupation as an obstetrician. My work makes life worth living. It is hard to imagine a greater joy than delivering a newborn baby into its mother's arms. I seldom lose a patient to death. When something goes wrong, I am able to concentrate my energy and perform the healing rituals silently.

Noni warned me about healing those that were meant for death. Death would not take kindly to me saving those that were meant for his harvest. She taught me the signs of his presence. The temperature in the room rising along with an unbearable heaviness that I'm sure no one else can feel but me. It feels like the walls of the room are squeezing my chest … like I'm suffocating.

Sometimes there are other signs. The one I look forward to is the flicker of the light that bursts over the patient. The body usually remains alive for a little longer, but the soul is gone. The reason I like the flash of light is because sometimes the nurses see it too. It makes me feel normal, which is something I have never really felt.

I know that most people do not want to be normal. People want to be special or extraordinary. Take it from me: different is not all it's cracked up to be.

Maybe I just feel that way because I feel so limited in my abilities here. If I were in my great grandmother's village, my talents would make me special in a good way. Here they make me a circus side show freak. That's why no one knows, not even my closest friends.

Right now, all I know is that seeing Marco after all these years would make it better. I know he is the key to this vision. I just have no idea why.

Oh Bartender, My Bartender

Adriano, the bartender, is out of place in this small town. He belongs on a runway or in a movie. I watched as he gently placed a raspberry lemon drop on the bar. I take a small sip, and before I am finished swallowing, he speaks.

"It's good?" he asked, curiously with his thick Brazilian accent. *Oh* … how I missed that sensual accent.

"Yes, very good, thank you," I answered, as I ran my finger around the wet edge of the glass. I looked down at my finger and wished that I had gotten them gelled longer and painted red instead of the plain clear polish on my clinically short nails. Unfortunately having long sexy nails is not really a possibility in my job. That would not go over well during a pap smear.

He turned and continued his work of tidying up the bar. He was facing the opposite end of the bar restacking clean glasses and I took the opportunity to stare … at his butt. I know slap my hand—chastise me. I will happily take the punishment. His body is hard not to stare at; drawing my eyes to it like they are no longer under my control. He is tall and muscular. His work uniform accentuates his form; showing off his athletic thighs and perfect round backside. I squirmed as I imagined sinking my teeth into it.

These primal urges seething to the surface of my normally proper mind are definitely beyond my control. They are totally irrational thoughts.

"Biddy, what have you been up to this week?" Poppy snapped her fingers in front of my face trying to get my attention. "Girl, you better stop staring so hard at that boy. Rhett will be jealous."

Rhett is my longtime boyfriend. We have known each other most of our lives. Our relationship was a solid one, based on friendship and mutual respect. I looked over at Rhett and he was still talking to Garrison. I highly doubted that Rhett even noticed me looking at the bartender's backside. He was locked up in a sports conversation. Garrsion, who is engaged to Dixie, liked to talk. The girl with the snapping fingers, Poppy, is the eternal bachelorette of our little group. Poppy likes dating men—lots of men. If you looked up the word *loose* in the dictionary, you would find her picture. I had the feeling that Poppy was just waiting for Rhett to break up with me. The only reason I maintain a friendship with her is because of Dixie. We are friends by association. Tolerance is my frame of mind around Poppy.

Poppy dated Rhett in high school but dumped him when she got to college. She was across the country and was sure that a long distance relationship would never work when there were so many cute fraternity boys for her to date. I know that Poppy regrets giving him up and I often wonder if Rhett feels the same way. He never talks about Poppy, but sometimes I catch him looking at her with a bit of yearning in his eyes. This was not something that I would ever ask him about; to be honest, I think it is perfectly reasonable to always have some level of emotional attachment to your first love. I certainly still did.

Just the slightest thought about Marco and my heart beats a little faster. I have resigned myself to living with the hole in my heart and the absence of the one man who could make me complete again.

But right now, in this moment in the bar I am feeling things that seem unnatural. I look back at Adriano.

"Can you blame me? Look at him." I discreetly motioned for my friends to look at the yummy bartender. The three of us ogle his body with our eyes then giggle as we take another sip of our drinks.

"How's it going at the hospital?" Poppy asked, trying to bring me into their conversation.

"Fine, I guess. It's been kind of slow. Not too many deliveries this week, just three so far." I delivered two girls and a boy this week. All of them were delivered successfully with no problems. It was the kind of week I liked. "Rhett's been under a bit more stress than me, but of course that is to be expected when you're trying to cure cancer." His field was downright depressing but fulfilling when he could help a patient into cancer remission.

I looked across the bar at Rhett. He is one of two oncologists at the small town hospital and is always busy. Rhett looked up at the same time and smiled. He is very handsome, just short of six foot and slim.

We lost contact after high school but met again during our

medical residencies; ending up at the same hospital in Texas. We provided moral support to each other throughout the long hours in the strenuous learning environment but never really discussed starting a relationship with each other. One night when I was having a particularly hard time with my attending physician, Rhett held me and listened as I cried. When I stopped sobbing, he wiped my face with the sleeve of his shirt and kissed me. It was tender and sweet. From that moment on, we were together.

Rhett and none of my other friends, for that matter, know about all of my special talents. They know that I have creepy dreams that sometimes come true, but it is more like a party trick to them than a psychic ability.

When Rhett has a head cold or some other illness, I pamper him with massages and perform the healing rituals silently. He thinks I am just being attentive. He always wakes up in the morning feeling better and makes some comment about having a strong immune system. I just smile and agree with him.

"When are you two going to get married?" Dixie teased. "You've been engaged for two years. Don't you think it's time? You're not getting any younger." Poppy perked up at the topic of conversation and leaned in closer to catch my answer.

"I'm just not ready for the wedding," I explained. I could never quite explain why I was not ready to get married. In a month, I'll be turning thirty-three-years-old. It is a perfectly acceptable age to get married. I have a secure career and Rhett's practice is thriving. We both have nice incomes. There is really no good reason not to get married—except that I just don't want to right now.

"What's the hold up?" Dixie pushed for more explanation. Dixie and Garrison are engaged and planning a summer wedding. It is going to be one of those extravagant Southern weddings. Everything in Texas is really bigger.

Ugh... I hate discussing this with Poppy hanging on my every word for some detail that will make it seem like Rhett and I are not happy. What can I say, I love Rhett, he is my best friend. I should want to marry him.

"I'm just not ready ... end of story, okay?" I take a large swig from my martini glass finishing it completely and placed the empty glass back on the bar.

Adriano leans on the bar with both hands and looks across at me. His shirt sleeves are rolled up half-way up his well-developed arms and his bartender's towel is flung over his shoulder. His eyes are mesmerizing. I am caught up for a moment as if I was under a predator's thrall. He smiles a toothy grin showing the full complement of his straight white teeth. His skin looks so smooth. I wonder how he would react if I touched his face or better yet one of his biceps.

"You want something else?" he asked, interrupting my scandalous thoughts. I feel my cheeks blush as I realize he has caught me staring at him. I definitely want something else from him, but I would never dare say that out loud, especially to a complete stranger. Well, maybe with several more martinis. *What's he putting in these drinks?*

"I'll have another one of these." I pointed to the glass in front of me. It is so unlike me to be so easily distracted by a man's

15

physical appearance. I am the kind of woman that is usually more attracted to a man with a big brain. Rhett has both qualities. He is definitely handsome and intelligent. I really should not be thinking steamy thoughts about this young man in front of me, but I cannot help myself. He must be at least ten years younger than me. He is practically illegal as far as I am concerned.

Adriano places another raspberry lemon drop martini in front of me on the bar. He also slides a napkin under the drink this time to prevent the wet ring that would occur when I lifted the full martini glass.

I hear Poppy and Dixie discussing colors and flowers for Dixie's wedding; I nod occasionally to encourage their conversation without having to fully participate.

I watch as Adriano opens two long neck bottles of beer and serves Rhett and Garrison. Rhett lifts the bottle of beer to his full lips and swallows. His Adam's apple bobs as the cold beer slides down his throat. He winks at me when he places the beer back down on the bar, letting me know that he has noticed me watching him.

Adriano seeing this slowly turns and stares at me. He has no way of knowing that this man is my boyfriend. Rhett has not touched me since we walked into the bar as a group. I smile at Rhett and look away from Adriano towards the girls. I wonder what Adriano is thinking right this minute. Through my peripheral vision I can see him staring at me as he takes a sip from a glass of water. He licks his bottom lip as he places the glass back down on the lower bar shelf.

I join the conversation about the upcoming wedding. "Have you ordered your dress?" I asked.

"Yes, and I've picked out yours, too." Dixie answered. "You both need to go into Kiki's Bridal Boutique for your dress fitting. We only have six months till the wedding." Poppy and I both looked at each other and wrinkle our noses in distaste. We both hate bride's maid's dresses just like every other woman who has ever had to wear one. The three of us laughed. "I promise you'll both like it."

We discuss more details about the wedding. Poppy and I are more interested in planning some fun girlfriend time. Like bridesmaids' luncheons, bridal showers, and especially a Bachelorette party weekend down on Bourbon Street.

The phone in the back pocket of my jeans vibrates. I pull it out and read the text message from Rhett. I don't look up at him, sensing that he is trying to send me a covert message.

The message reads: *Ready to go home? You start the good-byes.*

I nodded and put the phone back into my pocket. Rhett was not good at ending conversations, especially with Garrison. He likes that I do not mind looking like the party pooper.

"That was a text from my office manager. She's reminding me about an early morning meeting. I have to go home and get some sleep," I interrupt Dixie and Poppy discussing wedding cake flavors. It was still early in the evening, and I was not sure why Rhett wanted to leave so soon, but in a way I was happy that I was going to be separated from this strange pull I was feeling towards the bartender.

"You sure?" Poppy asked.

"Yeah, I have to be up early and it's already past my bed-time," I replied.

We perform our ritual group hug and make plans to meet for lunch one day next week. I walk away from my friends towards Rhett's seat at the corner of the bar.

"Rhett, you ready to take me home?" I asked, already fully aware of the answer.

"Already," he asked, whining. "Okay … I guess so."

I raised one eyebrow and I smiled at his weak protest. In some ways he is like a little boy, but I guess most men are.

Rhett waved to Adriano to get his attention. "We need to close out our tabs. Put her drinks on my bill … we're going home." Rhett slid his arm around my waist and pulled me in for a kiss on the lips.

I looked at Rhett a bit confused by this uncharacteristic display of possessiveness. Why did he feel it necessary to tell Adriano that he is taking me home? And why did it bother me that he said that?

Adriano totaled the bill and Rhett paid with cash leaving a generous tip.

"Let's go, sweetheart," Rhett said, grabbing my hand as he walked toward the door, his grip tight around my fingers.

"Goodnight," I called back to my friends. Garrison joined Dixie and Poppy. I looked back at Adriano. He was watching me again. We made eye contact and he smiled as Rhett pulled me out of the door. I really liked that smile. It was the smile of a man who knew that he made another man wrought with jealously over his mate. It was predatory and primal and utterly sexy.

"Why'd you tell the bartender you were taking me home," I asked Rhett.

"Huh?" He wrinkled his forehead in confusion. Maybe he had done it subconsciously. "What are you talking about?"

"You made a point of telling him that I was going home with you." I crossed my arms over my chest.

"Well, you are!" He shrugged and then pressed the unlock button on the car remote.

"You've never done anything like that before." I shook my head, beginning to wonder if he is jealous because of the excessive amount of time I had spent staring at Adriano's perfect body, but he had been pretty occupied in conversation all night; I did not think he had noticed. "Were you jealous?"

"No, not jealous," he denied. "Just letting him know that you were taken; that boy spent the whole night staring at you." He emphasized the word boy, letting me know that he also thought Adriano was too young to pay any attention to me. Rhett opened the car door for me and I slid inside.

What? He spent the whole night staring at me. Usually men stare at Poppy when we were out not at me. I could not help but smile at the thought of Adriano staring at me when I was not looking. It excited me right down to my core. Rhett got in the car and pulled out of the parking lot onto the street.

"Why was he staring?" I asked, curiously. Not that I really expected Rhett to know the answer. How can he know what another man was thinking? A better question would have been: Why do you think he was staring? I rested my head on the window gazing into the night and watched the stars in the clear night sky above us.

Rhett sighed. "I've failed you … haven't I?" He reached out to grab my hand. "I don't tell you often enough how beautiful you are."

I never really thought of myself as beautiful. I'm average height and at a healthy weight, but by no means skinny. Curvy maybe. *Who am I kidding?* I have lots of curve. I have long curly brown hair that is a bit unruly in the heat and humidity of the South, many days I just wear it in a ponytail. My blue grey eyes are well set against my olive skin. I feel that physically I was okay. My job was the only thing about me that I felt was above average, especially with my healing ability.

"I know that you think I'm beautiful …" I stopped midsentence. I wanted to say that he loved me and so if he thinks I am beautiful that in some way it did not count. I know it would hurt his feelings so I stopped talking.

"Biddy, do you know how much I love you?"

"I love you, too," I replied simply. What he did not understand was that I loved him as my best friend. It was not the same type and intensity of feelings that I felt and on some level still feel for Marco.

"You didn't answer my question," he clarified. "I was asking if you understand how much I love you."

"Oh …" I was confused. I thought it was just his way of saying he loved me. "I know you love me, Rhett. Love is kind of hard to quantify."

"You are my best friend and I would do anything for you," he said, pushing a stray strand of hair behind my ear. "There is something I want from you."

"What might that be?" I asked.

"I want to set a date for our wedding." He looked at me with his beautiful blue eyes and waited for a reply.

I do not want to get married right now. After seeing Adriano in the bar tonight I knew that I was not ready. I was not sure if it's because of the strange feelings of attraction or of the way he reminds me of Marco. Why couldn't he just be happy with the way things are? Why isn't living together enough for Rhett?

"Why can't we just keep things the way they are?" I asked.

"Because we've been engaged forever … it's time to get married." He stared at me waiting for an answer. The right answer. I knew he was being jealous of the handsome bartender, although he had denied it before.

"You are jealous because a man was staring at me?"

"It wasn't just that he was looking at you … men do that all the time. There was something different about it. You were ogling him. The heat coming off of the two of you was palpable. Even Garrison commented about it." Rhett and I stared at each other for what seemed like forever. "If you don't want to marry me then maybe we shouldn't be together anymore." The look on his face was serious and disappointed. He was in pain.

I focused on the anguish in his eyes. He does not deserve to be in pain and I despise myself for being the cause. Rhett had always been there for me and had treated me better than I deserved.

"Okay." I nodded, as I close my eyes and kissed his lower lip. He smiled and sighed in relief. I figured if I did not agree to marry him soon we would end up apart. I did not really want to get married, but I did not want to lose my best friend either. It was quite selfish of me, really. I wanted to have the security and companionship he so deftly supplied without making the ultimate commitment. "I have one condition."

"How can you have any conditions?" It was more of a statement than a question. "You've made me wait this long." He emphasized his last statement; laying blame on me for his torment. He looked over at me and I smiled. "Okay, Biddy. I give up. What is your condition?"

"My condition is that we elope. I don't want all the fuss. No big wedding." I didn't think that he would mind this condition. It would allow him to have what he wanted sooner and with less drama. He smiled. It was clear that he liked the idea; just as I expected he would.

"Sounds great. When and where?" he asked.

"I'll have to schedule a vacation and set up for someone to cover my patients. I imagine you'll have to do the same. I can probably work something out for next week. Want to go to Vegas?"

"I think I can clear most of my appointments and find someone to cover the rest." He leaned over and kissed me. "Let me take care of the plans. Just let me know as soon as you've decided which days you want to go and I'll arrange everything."

Distraction

My black BMW seemed to drive itself down Main Street toward my office on West Canal. I slowed the car as I reached the intersection of Main and Kildare. It was not unusual to see people out jogging, but this morning my eyes caught a glimpse of someone different. He was running towards the intersection and stopping on the sidewalk to assess the safety of crossing the street. It only took one moment for me to recognize the man. Adriano. *Thank You, Lord!* His chest was bare and glistening with a layer of sweat.

It was only seven o'clock in the morning and it was a warm January day. Yes, in the South there are plenty warm January days. These days are also typically filled with unbearable humidity that discourages the average person from exercising outside but here he was running with no shirt and looking even better than I remembered. His body was just as muscular as I had imagined it would be and the muscles moved under his skin fluidly.

The intersection was not busy. My traffic light was still red and I watched as he jogged across the road in front of me. His gaze flicked to my car. Our eyes met and we maintained eye contact until he was fully across the intersection. His gaze, those eyes, promised so much. I swear time stopped and stood still allowing me to prolong the glorious moment.

I smiled—the entire day. I couldn't help but smile. His image kept popping into my head at the most inopportune times. Several times while examining my patients, I caught myself day-dreaming. My office staff even commented on my unusual mood. It's not that I am not normally cheerful, but this mood was more ethereal giddiness. Unnatural. This was what I imagined it would be like to be high on drugs, but without any bad side effects.

I managed to almost make it through the entire day without thinking about my wedding plans. Operative word…almost.

The cat was let out of the bag when Rhett called Claire, my office manager, and asked if I had scheduled time off for the elopement. Claire is fifty-eight years old and was the previous OB/GYN's office manager before I bought his practice. She is short and has a body the shape of an apple. Her hair is dyed a bright shade of red and is cut into a short smooth bob. She moved her thick black framed glasses down the bridge of her nose and raised one eyebrow in my direction. With that one look I knew I was in trouble.

"Dr. Elliot," Claire called out across the desk where I was making notes in a patient's chart. "Dr. Foret wants to know what day you'll be eloping?" The older woman smiled and pushed the phone closer to me.

"Oh crap! I totally forgot to look at my calendar," I whispered to Claire. "Can we fix up a vacation for next week?" Claire flipped through the office appointment book. It was not very busy for next week. There was only one woman due to deliver that week. I don't believe in scheduling C-section deliveries. I encouraged my patients to deliver naturally if possible.

"I could manage rescheduling your appointments and I'll call Dr. Adamson to arrange for him to cover deliveries and emergencies. You'll owe him." Claire had it under control pointing to January 16th on the calendar. I reluctantly picked up the phone.

"Sweetheart, we can leave on the sixteenth and I can clear seven days." Claire stood across the desk from me and smiled slyly. I could see her green spearmint gum sticking out between her teeth as she smiled.

"Sounds great, I'll book a flight and make all the arrangements. You just need to pack a bag." Rhett said.

"Okay, I can handle that."

"One more thing," he paused. I could sense some apprehension. "Dixie is throwing us a party on the fifteenth to celebrate."

"Argghh!" I exhaled loudly from frustration. This is exactly the kind of thing I was trying to avoid. How did Dixie know about our plans to elope? Why couldn't he turn Dixie down when she offered throwing the party? "Dixie was upset that she had to hear about our plans from Garrison. Why didn't you call anyone?" I reached into my pocket and looked at my cell phone. I had eleven missed calls. Dixie and Poppy would be on a rampage. They will think I lied to them last night about not being ready to marry Rhett.

"We are *eloping,* Rhett. It is supposed to be a secret wedding. That is the whole point of eloping. You are a genius. I didn't think I needed to explain it to you." I say each word in hard staccato and an obviously angry tone. "I have to get back to my patients."

"I didn't realize you wanted to keep it a secret. I love you.

I'll see you tonight."

"Whatever!" I handed the phone receiver back to Claire and let my head fall onto the countertop with a loud thump.

"Don't be mad at him, honey. He can't read your mind." Claire gently placed the phone down. My right eye started twitching and one of those pin point headaches started to develop right behind my eyeball. I pushed my index finger into my eyelid to put pressure on the pain. I am aware of the fact that Rhett cannot read my mind. In fact, I am grateful that he cannot. It would only lead to pain, if he knew that I really am not ready for this marriage.

"What room is my next patient in?" I asked, as I pressed my finger further into my twitching eyelid. I was not going to discuss my problems with my staff or anyone else for that matter. The pain behind my eye disappeared. Being a natural healer had its perks.

"Room four," a high pitched voice announced. It sounded like one of the new student nurses who was here fulfilling her clinical observations. Great, everyone in the office now knew I was eloping.

When I finished seeing my afternoon appointments, I noticed a vase filled with an assortment of tropical flowers sitting on my office desk. I searched the beautiful arrangement for a note or card, but there was none. Guess he just couldn't think of the words to apologize. How could I stay mad at him?

On my way home I drove past the Blue Crab Pub, the bar we had been to the night before. There were no cars parked on the street. It was early and I knew there would not be many people inside. I decided to drive this way to determine if Adriano was working. I really wanted to see him again. There's was just something drawing me to him. A small black motorcycle parked in the alley on the side of the bar caught my eye. It looked like something he would drive. Sleek and sensual. The bike was a definite turn on. I imagined what it would be like to ride behind him wrapping my arms around his hard body. I wanted to park my car and walk into the bar and well … I was not sure where to take it from there. I decided it was best just to keep on driving. For now… at least.

The Elopement Party

This party was a bad idea. I was not enjoying all of this attention. It was formal dress and I selected a black and white cocktail dress with thick black raised floral embroidery along the hem. I styled my long brown hair with big soft curls and applied the requisite smoky eye for the evening.

Dixie had invited way too many people. Everyone was dressed appropriately except for Poppy, which was no surprise to anyone. Poppy has a distinctive style. The style screamed high end call girl. Her long blonde hair was in a twisted up-do, and her dress was skin tight gold metallic fabric; her ample breasts spill out of the top of the dress. I swear a couple of times I thought I saw a nipple peeking over the top. When I looked at her, it was like staring into the sun.

I played my part and mingled with the well wishers; smiling especially when Rhett was around. Most of the guests including Rhett were pretty well on their way to alcohol poisoning. I stopped after one celebratory glass of champagne. Somehow I managed to keep up the façade of bridal happiness. Tomorrow we would be married. Hopefully our lives would just return to normal. Normal was good. It wasn't a dream come true. It wasn't Adriano and it definitely wasn't Marco, but I had learned to live with being as normal as possible.

When the last guest left, I searched the house for Rhett so we could go home and rest before our flight in the morning. I opened the door to Dixie's bedroom to grab my handbag. The room was dark, but there was light coming through the crack at the threshold of the door to the bathroom inside the master suite. The sound of voices coming from the bathroom was intriguing. I stepped closer and put my ear to the door. The sound was Poppy giggling. I had heard that particular giggle before. Poppy was in the process of getting laid. Some women moan during sex, but not Poppy; she giggles.

Suddenly, I lost my balance, and my shoulder leaned further into the door and it swung open. The lovers forgot to lock the door. I fell on the white ceramic tile of the bathroom and looked up to see Rhett giving Poppy a breast exam with his mouth. Apparently, his oral cavity doubled as a mammography machine. Such a dedicated oncologist.

I am up on my feet before anyone can say anything. The mixture of emotions running through me is confusing. Anger at the betrayal, yet a little relief as well. I pulled the engagement ring off my finger and flung it at the two of them. It landed right in Poppy's ample cleavage. Rhett grabbed the ring and turned to me, but I was already backing out of the door. I had my car keys out and was inside my car and on the street before anyone else in the house knew what is happening. I treasured my privacy and I hated the idea of this betrayal becoming a public display.

I drove back towards our apartment, too angry to cry. *What a jack-ass!* He guilted me into agreeing to marry him and then two seconds later he was fondling his old flame. Of course, it was what I always expected from Poppy. It was no less shocking when I saw it with my own two eyes. I wondered how long this had been going on. My intuition, which is seldom wrong, told me that tonight was the first time he had betrayed me. I'd caught many boyfriends cheating through my dreams and intuition. It's was a useful talent. Rhett had never given me any reason to think that this had happened before.

To get to my apartment I had to drive in front of the bar where Adriano was working. I slowed down as I passed by the Blue Crab Pub's entrance. The small black motorcycle was sitting in the same spot as the last time I drove past. This time I parked my car across from the bar and found my way inside. I was still not sure what I was going to do or why I felt compelled to see him again.

The bar was empty except for a few couples sitting at the small intimate tables in the corners, but the bar stools were deserted. Adriano was wiping down the area getting ready to close up soon. It is almost two in the morning and that was the bar's usual closing time. I took a seat on one of the stools at the bar as Adriano turned to me and placed my favorite martini on the bar.

"You remembered…" I said, taking in his body with my eyes. He was wearing his bartender's uniform of tight black slacks and a white button down shirt rolled up to his elbows. I smiled as I thought about the day he jogged past me in all his sweaty glory. I slowly sipped the drink as I waited for his reply.

"How could I forget? You are the sexiest woman to ever

step foot into this bar," Adriano proclaimed boldly with that thick Brazilian accent that felt like velvet wrapping around my erogenous zones.

"You must be thinking of the blonde that was in here with me the other night," I said acidly.

"No, she's not my type." He shook his head in disgust. "Too slutty. She tried to take me home with her that night."

"I like your character judging ability. I just caught that bitch with her big fake breasts in my fiancé's mouth."

"He doesn't deserve you." Adriano leaned his elbow on the bar and watched me drink his delicious concoction.

"Want to go to Vegas?" I smiled. "My treat," It just slipped out of my mouth before I even realized what I am saying. I was not even sure if I have actually said it out loud; until I noted the shocked but satisfied look on his face.

Well hell. I had the next week off and I was not waiting around to hear Rhett's excuses. I was angry. Rhett pushed me. He used guilt to get me to agree to marry him when I wasn't ready. At this moment I felt that Poppy and Rhett can have each other.

"I was supposed to elope tomorrow, but that won't be happening and I have a week's vacation and two plane tickets in my bag," I explained.

Adriano leaned down over the bar and smiled seductively. His biceps bulged as he placed his hands on the bar and involuntarily flexed the muscles.

"You don't even know me and you want to take me on your honeymoon?" His face was almost touching mine as he moved closer to me. The scent of him was woodsy and all male. He overcame my senses as he continued to move closer.

"I'm feeling a bit adventurous at the moment." I licked a drop of the sweet drink off my bottom lip and watched as his eyes dropped to my mouth and slowly made their way back up to my eyes. He leaned back and folded his arms across his broad chest.

"I could be the big bad wolf," he said in a gruff tone, as he pushed his long dark hair out of his eyes. "Are you sure you want to take that chance?"

"You look more like a jungle cat to me." I tossed back the rest of my drink and placed the glass back onto the bar. Adriano's smile grew showing his perfect teeth, which upon closer examination revealed that his canines did look unusually sharp.

"Okay, when do we leave?" His angular jaw flexed drawing more of my attention to his tempting mouth.

"In about five hours."

"Do I need to pack anything special?" he asked.

"Whatever you think you'll need for a week in Vegas." The alcohol was providing me with a bit more courage that I would usually have in this type of environment. I leaned over the bar and brushed my lips slowly across Adriano's mouth. "Are you ready to close this place up for the night?"

Adriano looked around the bar; all the patrons had left without notice during our conversation. He walked around the bar and pulled all the shades down and locked the front door. I confidently followed him out of the back door in to the dark alley.

"So what's your name?" He asked as he handed me his helmet.

"Biddy Elliot. What's yours?" I knew his name was Adriano but I figured it was polite to return the question.

"Adriano Medeiros." He turned and straddled the bike and I hopped on behind him. He pulled out of the alley onto the quiet street. I wrapped my arms around him assuming we were driving to his apartment. I pressed the palms of my hands flat to his hard warm abdomen.

Adriano's apartment was on the third floor of an apartment complex that looked like it was built in the 1970's. The exterior was white vinyl siding and an orange brick. The black wrought iron staircases wrapped around the corners of the building.

He apologized for the broken elevator as we hiked up the metal stair case. Then he took my hand and led me to his door. A small brass plate screwed to the apartment door read 3C. He unlocked the door and turned on the lights. The apartment looked like it hadn't been renovated since the 1970s, either. There was bright orange shag carpeting in the living room and the walls are covered in dark wood paneling. The furniture consisted of mix and match pieces that he probably found at thrift stores or on the side of the curb. I watched him as he cleaned up empty dishes and food packages that he has left strewn across the various pieces of furniture. There were no empty beer cans so apparently the bartender was not a big drinker himself.

"Sorry for the mess," he said. "I wasn't expecting company."

"No problem." I shrugged and sat in his overstuffed brown leather recliner. "Do you live alone?"

"Yeah, I moved here a few weeks ago."

"From Brazil?"

"How'd you know?" he asked, sounding surprised by my correct guess.

"Your accent gave you away. I spent a few months there a long time ago." I smiled fondly remembering my time there, especially my time with Marco.

"Cool. I'll go pack." His reply seemed a bit odd. I expected him to act more interested in the fact that I had spent time in his home country. He should have at least asked me what city I visited.

Adriano slipped into the bedroom in his tiny apartment. He reappeared after only five minutes with a duffle bag. We left the apartment and made our way back down to the parking lot and the motorcycle. Adriano drove us back to the bar and dropped me off next to my car. He followed me to the apartment I shared with Rhett. Once there I showed him where he could park his bike while we are gone.

There were no sounds coming out of the apartment. I hoped that Rhett had not come home yet. My bag was already packed; I just wanted to slip inside, grab the bag, and get the airline tickets. I was nervous about opening the door. My hands were shaking and I missed the key hole a few times. What if Rhett was in there with

Poppy or even worse, what if he is in there alone? I handed the keys to Adriano and he unlocked the door and turned the knob. There were no lights on inside the apartment. Adriano followed me around as I checked the various rooms for any sign of Rhett's presence. A sweep of the rooms revealed nothing. He had not come home. I audibly exhaled in relief after checking the bedroom.

"This is a nice apartment." Adriano stepped closer to me. "I see you received the flowers," he said as he wrapped his hand around my waist.

"The flowers?" I looked at the vase on the table and then back at the beautiful man holding me possessively. "You sent me the flowers?"

That rat fink Rhett had let me go on and on about the flowers and how wonderful he was for sending them to me to apologize for blabbing about our elopement. He never once tried to correct my mistake. I actually apologized for getting mad at him. Of all the nerve, what kind of man takes credit for another man's romantic gesture?

"Yes, I wanted to give you a gift," he leaned down and kissed the spot behind my ear that makes me shiver in delight. "Do you like them?" His warm breath on my neck as he spoke increased the sensitivity of every nerve ending in my body.

"Oh, yes." I moaned not sure if I was really answering his question about the flowers are just giving my verbal approval to his ability to make my body ache with the touch of his breath on my skin.

"The bed looks very inviting." He gently pushed me onto

the bed and proceeded to take off his shirt. I watched him undress. He held my gaze with his; never breaking visual contact. Each article of clothing he removed revealed more muscle and smooth dark skin. *Okay maybe I broke eye contact.* His chest had a small patch of black hair right in the middle and then there was the enticing trail of dark hair that ran from his belly button down to his happy place. His pants hit the floor. He stood before me in complete nakedness … and he didn't disappoint. He was tanned over every inch of his body and muscles bulged and curved in all the right places. He lay on the bed and leaned against the fluffy pillows. I can't imagine the expression on my face at this point because I was so shocked by what he had just done.

"Your turn."

"My turn for what?" I asked. I knew what he meant but I wasn't ready for that yet. Either my shyness was kicking in or the alcohol was wearing off.

"Undress for me." His tone was commanding. He said it with authority as if there was no chance that he would be refused. He might be the big bad wolf after all. This was moving way faster than I expected. I fully planned on having sex with him. Lots of it, but I was thinking we would wait until we got to Las Vegas. I didn't want to do it here in the bed I shared with Rhett.

"Here's the thing. I don't know anything about you yet." I twisted my hands together exposing my nervousness at the situation I found myself in.

"I thought you were feeling adventurous?" His voice softened my reserve. He watched me as he leaned on his elbow; his perfectly proportioned bicep bulging under the force of his flex and the weight of his body.

"Yeah … you know what happens in Vegas stays in Vegas." Maybe they don't know that slogan in Brazil.

Adriano reached across the bed and unzipped my dress. He ran his warm fingers down the length of my back. The sensation created by his fingers was like fire licking at my skin. *Oh what the hell*. I stood to slide my body out of the dress. Just as my dress hit the floor; the bedroom door flung open and Rhett stood in the doorway in a drunken stupor flanked by Dixie and Garrison. They were holding him up under his arms and it looked like they were struggling to keep him in a vertical position. In his drunken condition he must have felt like dead weight.

"Great, this is all I need." I slid the dress back on and zipped myself up quickly. Embarrassed that my best-friend's fiancé had just seen me in my undies and that I had been caught in a compromising position by what felt like everyone I knew.

"I knew it!" Rhett exclaimed. "I knew you wanted to sleep with this guy." Garrison and Dixie quickly backed out of the room, but not before Dixie gestured a thumbs up and mouthed the words, "Oh my God!" They ran to the apartment door and let themselves out; the door slamming behind them. I will have to remember to thank her later for deserting me in my most desperate hour of need.

"I'm not talking about this with you right now, especially after what I caught you doing with that … that … skank," I spit out the words. My body temperature must have hit its boiling point because I could feel the skin on my neck and face turning red. I

picked up Adriano's clothes and tossed them onto the bed next to him. "Get dressed, Adriano, we're leaving."

Adriano was apparently born without an embarrassment gene because he stood up right in front of Rhett in all his naked glory before proceeding to put on his pants. It was more likely that Adriano knew he was muscled perfection and did not mind everyone knowing it. The fact that he was fully aroused added to my embarrassment, but he was quite impressive. If he was trying to make Rhett feel insignificant, I had the feeling it worked. Rhett's mouth was wide open. I leaned forward and pushed his chin up. He smacked away my hand and grunted something under his breath.

"Is this want you want?" Rhett asked pointing to Adriano; who was only missing his shirt now. "He is just some young boy who tends bar. He can't provide you with what you need."

"Yes, at the moment he is what I want." How dare Rhett insinuate that I needed a man to take care of me? Yes, it's true that emotionally I had relied on him for comfort and friendship, but financially I could take care of myself.

Adriano finished getting dressed and pulled me towards the door. He lifted my luggage and I grabbed my purse with the plane tickets.

"Biddy, please let me explain." Rhett tried grabbing my arm, so I would stay and listen. Before I could even respond, Adriano punched Rhett in the face. His nose was crooked and bleeding.

Wow! I smiled. I wanted to do that, but did not have the nerve. Adriano was downright barbaric. I liked it. I liked it a whole bunch.

"Let's go, Gatinho." Adriano opened the door and we left Rhett holding his bloody nose. Adriano slid behind the wheel of my car.

"That was amazing," I said, impressed by Adriano's macho bravado and raw masculinity. He did not talk much and what little he did say revolved around whether or not I was feeling alright and if I was sure I wanted to take him to Vegas. He focused on the road and getting us to the airport. Oddly enough I felt safe with him, even though he was still a complete stranger.

The Odd Couple

The taxi dropped us off at the front entrance of our
hotel. Adriano carried our bags and followed me to the front desk.
We were both still wearing our clothes from the night before. I
checked into the suite, obtaining two keys. I handed one of them to
Adriano. We continued to the elevator following the bell boy and
our luggage to the suite. The bell boy explained that the room was
1,500-square-feet of arc shaped luxury with several large windows
with views of the Las Vegas skyline. The furniture having modern
lines was covered in lavish animal prints. The huge king size bed
was draped in blood red bedding with black and white zebra trim.
The matching draperies were operated with a slim silver remote
control. One look at the room and I could only think of one word—
Elvis.

We were both hungry from our flight so we agreed to go
to dinner. Entering the casino, I was instantly over stimulated by
the multicolored flashing lights and the various dinging bells and
machines. Adriano looked very comfortable. He must just be one of
those people who can fit in anywhere. He was wearing faded jeans
ripped over one knee and a tight black t-shirt. I, on the other hand,
looked like a private secretary in my grey pencil skirt and white
satiny blouse. Adriano insisted that my outfit was extremely sexy.

When I had emerged from the bathroom, he groaned and muttered something in Portuguese that I did not understand, but it sounded intriguing.

The looks we were getting from the crowd were causing me some anxiety. I realized that we looked a bit mismatched. People were alright with seeing an older man with a young woman, but a younger man with an older woman still caused people to take double takes and stare.

"You realize I look like your older sister?" I huffed as I watched a group of young women stare at Adriano. I fought the urge to hand them a napkin to sop up all their drool.

"Gatinho, you worry too much," Adriano replied as he pulled me into the crowded elevator close to him and touched his mouth to my ear. "I'm here with you and I am not interested in any of these silly little girls." He slowly ran his hand down the length of my arm and wrapped his fingers around mine. "I want you."

Before I could respond, the elevator doors opened and we stepped out into the entrance of the roof top restaurant. We were greeted by an attractive brunette in a silver dress with a plunging neckline that showed off her breasts and her purple butterfly tattoo. She seated us at a small table near a picture window framing a spectacular view of the Vegas strip. I had lost total track of actual time, but it was dark outside, so the casinos were lit up with all their fanfare and magnificence. The hostess' silver dress reflected the numerous colors and created a walking disco ball. I realized that all the female staff were dressed this way. It created quite an effect on the restaurant's atmosphere.

Adriano ordered our drinks and then slid his hand over my fingers. His dark hair fell into his eyes as he focused his attention on me. This time I didn't restrain myself from touching his face. He said he wanted me. I had seen him naked. I think I'm entitled to touch his face whenever I want to. My hand moved to tenderly brush the silky black hair out of his line of vision. His copper eyes focused on mine. Then the strangest thought popped into my head. We would make beautiful babies. *Where did that come from? I immediately turned my head to break our stare and get the thought of babies out of my head. The dream I kept having of the little baby girl was hard to decipher. I wondered if it meant I would have a baby with Adriano.*

"What's wrong?" Adriano asked after I did not immediately return to gazing into his beautiful eyes.

"I was just having the strangest thoughts," I began to explain. "I was thinking...no never mind you really don't want to know."

"I want to know everything about you," he chuckled. "I've been having some unusual ideas, too."

"If you tell me yours, I'll tell you mine," I said, as I played with his hair.

"I've been thinking that I'm falling in love with you." He smiled gently and waited for my response.

In love with me. We've only known each other such a small fraction of time, but that first night in the bar, I felt something for him that I had not felt in a long time. Not since I was seventeen. I just thought it was an extreme case of lust. Although, I was just thinking about babies so is love so far off?

"Your turn, Gatinho." He was getting impatient waiting for me to mull over his declaration.

"Mine might scare you right out of falling in love." I paused for a moment to look at him and work up the courage to actually say the word baby to a man I hardly knew. This is ridiculous; I should want babies with Rhett. Rhett is the kind of man you have babies with, not Adriano. Adriano would be great for practicing making babies. "I was thinking that you and I would make beautiful babies together." I dropped my head avoiding his eyes. I fully expected him to run away screaming, but instead he moved his chair closer to mine and pulled my chin up with his hand forcing me to look at him. He didn't look scared; in fact, he looked happy. His fingers moved to wrap themselves into my long brown curls and he pulled me closer and gently parted my lips with his kiss. The kiss became more passionate and ended with me realizing that I had not been breathing for the entire length of it. Who needed to breathe when there were kisses like this? "So, I take it your interested in making babies."

"Very interested." His fingers gently brushed the length of my cheek and neck down into the opening of my silky blouse. His fingers slid back and forth over the skin between my breasts sending a shiver down my spine waking up the butterflies in my stomach.

"You remind me of someone I used to know." I wondered if that was the reason I was so physically, and I guess, emotionally attracted to him.

"Really, who might that be?" he asked as he took my hand and lightly kissed the inside of my wrist.

"A boy I knew when I was in Brazil. It was a long time ago, and he broke my heart."

"Well, I'll try to be more careful with it than he was, Gatinho." His lips moved from my wrist down to the palm of my hand.

"You keep calling me that. What does it mean?" I asked.

"Little cat," he said before slowly sipping from his glass of wine. "It's what men in my country call their women. It's like me calling you baby or sweetheart."

"This just seems crazy; we hardly know each other..." I said, shaking my head.

"Again with the worrying. We will have to break you from this useless habit," Adriano interrupted. "Let me explain something to you. I am very attracted to you physically. I think I might be in love with you. I can't explain it, but admit it, you feel drawn to me, too. I know you do. I can see it in your eyes and the way your body reacts to mine. That first night in the bar was torture because I wanted to climb over the bar and take you home, but I knew you were with him." Adriano said the last word with a bit of disgust.

"Rhett was jealous that night. He said he could feel the heat between us." But Rhett's jealousy was somewhat rational. I had been his for the past four years. I was pretty sure I knew what Adriano wanted to do with me, and it didn't seem quite so noble. *"May I ask you a question?"* He nodded in agreement. *"How old are you?"* Okay so the age difference was still bothering me.

"Twenty-six." I winced at the realization that he was six years younger than me. He placed his hand on my cheek and looked deep into my eyes. *"It's just a number, it doesn't mean anything."* Maybe he's just intrigued by the idea of dating or should I say sleeping with an older woman.

"You just look so much younger than that." He looked nineteen or twenty.

"Yeah, I know. I wish I looked older it would be easier to handle my father." He snapped bitterly. His body tensed and he pulled away from our intimate closeness. I did not respond to his comment immediately. My body ached as he withdrew his touch from me. The waitress approached our table and we ordered dinner. Once she was away from our table, I felt more comfortable approaching this new topic and his brooding mood.

"Do you have a difficult relationship with your father?" I asked.

"Yes, but I didn't mean to bring it up." He waved away the discussion. "It's not your problem. We're here to have fun."

"Is that the only reason you're here?"

"No, I have other plans." He smiled and I melted inside. I could feel that there was a little boy hurting inside of his muscular exterior.

"I would like to hear about it if you ever want to talk…"

"Listen, short story," he interrupted. "My father beat my mother and he favored my older brother. Me, he didn't care for much. My mother and sisters tried to protect me from him. I left home to protect them. I haven't seen them in months." He was clearly pained at having to speak about it out loud. I knew that he was holding back much more painful experiences.

"I'm sorry; you don't have to talk about it if you don't want to."

"Thank you," he sighed.

The rest of the evening was much like a regular date. I did most of the talking. I told him about my career, my family, and about my reservations about marrying Rhett. He listened intently, asking questions that made it seem like he was genuinely inter-ested. We ate and drank until we were both satiated and until I was quite tipsy. Sloppy drunk actually. When we stood to leave the restaurant, I knocked over a glass of wine and it spilled over the length of the white table cloth. My legs gave out and Adriano caught me up into his arms and carried me through the restaurant to the elevator and through the crowded casino. We were quite a spectacle. People turned to stare and some even stopped to ask if they could call an ambulance. Adriano explained to them politely that I was just drunk and that he was carrying me away to ravish me. We both laughed at the reactions this drew from the concerned tourists.

"Are you really planning on ravishing me in my condition?" I whispered innocently.

"I have a better idea," he whispered into my ear. "Let's get married."

"Didn't I just explain to you that I don't want to be married? I just dumped Rhett."

"Think about it, Gatinho. It's the perfect revenge. We go home and you're my wife, Rhett will be devastated. We can get a divorce whenever you're ready."

I must be extremely drunk because his idea actually sounded reasonable. "Okay, let's do it."

A taxi dropped us off in front of one of the many wedding chapels located in Las Vegas. The small white bricked storefront looked like it had seen better times. The sign on the double glass door indicated that it was open twenty-four hours. When Adriano opened one of the doors, the door chimed loudly announcing our entrance. The inside of the wedding chapel looked just like what I imagined it would. It resembled a small country church with five rows of wooden pews which created a very short aisle that led to a small stepped area where the marriages took place under a wrought iron arbor covered in plastic ivy and white taffeta ribbon. An old woman greeted us. She was short and wrinkly, but full of spunk.

No one without spunk could pull off the lavender bedazzled jump-suit she was wearing. Her face was done up with bright pink blush on both of her sagging cheeks. Her lipstick was bright red and there was some on her teeth. Her eyelids were covered in bright purple eye shadow and her head was covered with short tight blue curls.

"Well, hello lovebirds." The woman greeted us enthusi-astically. "My name is Cookie and I'll be your wedding organiz-er." She winked at me and leaned closer to prevent Adriano from hearing her next comment. "He's a little young for you honey, but he sure is a looker."

Great! Now the eccentric old lady who runs a Las Vegas twenty-four hour wedding chapel dressed in her outrageous Elvis style bedazzled jumpsuit is judging me. How dare she.

"Yeah, he's six years younger than me, and he's anatomi-cally perfect." I made a hand gesture like a proud fisherman who just caught the biggest fish of his life to give her some idea as to how perfect.

"You sure you can keep up with him, sweetie?" Cookie said with raised eyebrows. *My God, how old does she think I am?*

"I'll let you know if I need your help."

"Cookie, we'd like to get married…preferably tonight." Adriano interrupted, growing impatient with our muted conversa-tion.

"No duh, sonny. Follow me. I'll explain how this works."

We followed Cookie to a small podium where she explained the options available for wedding packages.

"We just want to get married, nothing fancy." *What am I saying; there is no possible way that anything that takes place here would be considered fancy.* Cookie's expression seemed disappointed. I guess she likes putting on a big show. Adriano smiled and leaned in close to Cookie and whispered something in her ear. She instantly looked happier. She walked away, humming a little tune. It sounded like Here Comes the Bride.

"What did you tell her?" I asked.

"I told her we wanted the Ultimate Wedding Package."

"Oh, no you didn't." I shook my head at him and threw my hands into the air.

"Yes, I want this to be special." He leaned in a kissed my forehead.

"We are only getting married to make Rhett jealous. Why does the ceremony have to be special?" I whined. Adriano's reaction was of instant hurt. He looked like a five-year-old whose balloon had just been popped. *Great now I hurt his feelings.*

"Because I want you to have a nice wedding. Is that so wrong? And you may not love me yet, but I do think I love you." He skimmed another sweet kiss across my forehead. "Please just go along with it for me?"

How could I resist. I nodded and leaned into his warm body. He held me tightly in his arms as I enjoyed the feeling of being with him.

"Hey, cougar bride. Come here." Cookie called me from inside a dressing room. Adriano's body shook with silent laughter. I guess he understood the terminology.

"Hey, it's not funny. It was your idea to marry an older woman." I rolled my eyes.

"Sorry, she's just so fun." He let me go and shoved me towards the dressing room with a quick smack on my backside. I turned and gave him the gimlet eye.

Cookie pulled me through the heavy white curtain into the small room with the three way mirror and a rack of wedding gowns. She was smiling wide as she yanked an old fashioned long sleeved white lace gown from the rack. It looked like something she would have worn sixty years ago.

"How about this one?" She held the dress up in front of me. *No way, Jose.* I glanced at the rack of dresses. There was nothing there that fit my simple taste in fashion, but there were a few unconventional dresses to choose from. *Okay if Adriano wants a wedding to remember, I'll give it to him.*

"No, how about the red one," I said, pointing to the outrageous gown. Cookie looked at me in complete shock.

"Are you sure?" she questioned as she lifted the dress from the rack and unzipped the side of the dress. I undressed and stepped into the blood red velvet evening gown. The dress was skin tight and the strapless heart shaped neckline gave the impression that I was more endowed in the bust that I actually was. The dress also sported a slit in the front that went straight up to my who-ha. Cookie slid a black and red lace garter up my thigh where the slit was and you could see the black lace peeking out from the dress. I slid my black heels back on my feet and stood straight to admire the transformation in the mirror.

"Hot damn!" Cookie exclaimed. Her dentures popped out of her mouth. She caught them in her hands. She slipped them back in. "Sorry about that."

"You think he'll like it?" I asked as I turned in the mirror to admire how the dress clung to my backside and accentuated my curves.

"He'll probably pass out." She handed me a bouquet of fake red roses. "Makes you look like you've got a butt like J-Lo." *Well, that is definitely better than having a butt like Jell-O.*

"Thanks, Cookie." I was starting to get into the spirit of this. "Will you take a picture of us during the ceremony? I handed her my cell phone. "I want to send this memory to some friends."

"Sure. Wait here until you hear the music and then come down the aisle." She walked through the white curtain and left me alone to wait for the music to start. The sound of an organ playing *Here Comes the Bride* made its way to the dressing room and I emerged on cue. I stepped through the door way and grabbed on the last pew as I stood there and stared at Adriano dressed in a black tuxedo. The tux fit him perfectly. He smiled and mouthed the word, "wow" as he stared back at me. I gathered my nerve and walked down the aisle and stood next to him. I reached out and pushed his chin up to close his mouth. He smiled back at the gesture.

"I take it you approve of my choice of dress?" I purred in

52

my best sex goddess impression.

"Hmmm," he moaned and mumbled something in Portuguese. By the look on his face, he was trying to figure out how to get me out of the dress.

"I'm really going to have to learn how to speak Portuguese, so I can understand you."

"Ahhmm." Cookie's husband cleared his throat to get our attention. "Are you ready to begin?" The old man looked nothing like Cookie. He was dressed in a light brown suit with a red bow-tie. He looked normal; bald and covered in liver spots. He proceeded with the ceremony, and before I knew it, I was saying "I do". Then it was time for the rings.

"Oh, we didn't think about rings," I exclaimed.

"No problem, I've got it covered." Adriano pulled a simple silver wedding band out of his pocket and placed it in my hand. "This one is for you to give to me."

I held the ring out as he held his left hand up for me to slide the ring onto his finger. Then I watched as he pulled a small gold ring off of his pinky finger and slid it onto the ring finger of my left hand. I looked down to examine the ring. There was something familiar about the symbols on the ring. The ring had a small cat among other swirling symbols. Cookie's husband pronounced us husband and wife and at that moment Adriano raised my face to his and gently kissed my lips.

"You're mine," he said softly as our lips parted from our first kiss as husband and wife.

"Well, now that I'm yours, what are you going to do with me?" I said putting my hands on my hips.

"I've got plans," he smiled. "The first of which involves that nice big bed in our hotel room."

We thanked Cookie and her husband, Roy. Adriano gave Cookie extra money for the red dress, so he could have the pleasure of taking it off of me when we were alone. And once we were back in the room that is just what he did. He unzipped the side zipper and pushed the dress to the floor.

"Undress me." He spoke softly as he looked over my body hungrily. I pulled the black t-shirt that he had changed back into over his head and then slowly ran my fingers over his collarbone and then down over his chest and flattened my hands over his hard abdomen. I looked up into his eyes and was taken aback by the way his eyes seemed reflective in the dark. He caught my reaction and instantly closed his eyes and moaned. "Keep going." He urged me to finish the job. I unbuttoned his jeans and slowly unzipped them, placing my hands inside the waistband and slid the jeans down towards the floor. He stepped out the jeans and lifted me onto the soft bed. He lifted the bedding for me to slide inside and he followed suit. The feeling of the cool sheets in contrast to Adriano's warm flesh on my bare skin was exhilarating. Adriano softly brushed his lips across mine until I opened my mouth to allow him to take the kiss further. The feel of his lips and tongue sent a tingling sensation over the entire length of my body. He slowly moved his kisses back up my neck close to my ear.

"This will only hurt a little," he whispered. Before I was even sure of what I heard him say, I felt his teeth sink into my shoulder as he punctured my skin.

"Adriano!" I screamed as the sharp pain burned through my skin. *Only hurt a little, was he joking.* I struggled to free myself from his mouth and arms, but the more I struggled the more it burned.

"Stop moving!" he demanded. "I'll make it better. I promise." He slowly licked the blood dripping from the wound. His tongue felt rough against my skin. Not like it felt when he kissed me. He took great care and pleasure in licking the wound; like it was something to be revered. As he finished licking and kissing my shoulder, he snuggled his face into my neck and made a strange guttural noise. It was the sound of satisfaction and total happiness. I was not sure what to make of what had just happened, but there was something so sensual about it, even though we had not had sex.

"Why'd you bite me?" I asked, bravely after he moved off to the side and was just laying there watching me.

"Because you are mine, Gatinho." He brushed his fingertip across my lower lip. "You are mine and we are now inseparable."

"How does you biting me make us inseparable?"

"Do you remember in the bar I told you that I was the big bad wolf?" He smiled as he pulled me closer.

"Yes, are you trying to tell me you really think you're a wolf?" I really should have thought a little more about marrying someone I didn't know. Of course, it would have helped if I would not have drunk so much wine. I lifted my body onto my elbows and tried to figure out where he was going with this.

"No, not a wolf," he said as he shook his head and the silky black hair fell into his eyes. "Do you remember what you said to me in response?"

"Yes, I said you look more like jungle cat." As I looked into his copper eyes and the light from the bedside lamp reflected in his irises, I realized that there was something special about him. "So you're telling me that you are a cat?"

"Not really." The corner of his mouth twitched like he was suppressing his desire to laugh. "I have the ability to shift into a black jaguar, but I am a man—a shape shifter." His expression was calm and serious, like what he was saying was the most natural thing in the world.

"That still doesn't explain why you bit me." Not that I believed his story yet, but there were things about me that were special, too. I was going to give him a chance to explain.

"I was marking you." He ran his fingers over the scar he left on my shoulder. My skin tingled under his touch. "This mark lets any other male shifter know that you are taken. No other man like me would dare touch you now. You are my mate. Mine. We are not only legally married by law of man, but by the law of the jungle."

"What about regular men?" I asked.

"They will just think you've been bitten by a large animal. It won't hold any significance to them, but if I ever catch you with another man," he paused to hold my head in his hands. "I will kill him. You are mine and only mine. You will be faithful to me do you understand?"

"I'm your wife, for now and unlike some people I know, I don't cheat. But I do need some proof of what you are telling me. You can't expect me to believe you turn into a jaguar without actually seeing it." He stood and bent to pick up his t-shirt off the floor.

"Put this on." He handed me the t-shirt. "Now, you must remain calm. I'm going to shift and you have to keep still and don't scream. Do you understand?"

I pulled on his t-shirt and nodded my head in agreement. I laid my head against the pillow to watch him. Before my eyes, his hands and feet changed into large black paws. He held up his hands to me so that I could see the large brown pads and sharp claws. He smiled and then there was a big black cat pacing in front of me. The change was so quick that if I had not of first seen him standing there with the paws I would have claimed it was some mind trick. He lifted his front paws onto the bed and jumped up beside me.

He was beautiful, and for some reason, I was not scared. He simply lay down and placed his giant head onto his stretched out arms and looked up at me. I sat there for a moment and surveyed him. His eyes were the same copper color. I reached out to touch the top of his head and he remained still. I slid my hand over his head and his fur was just as silky as his hair was when he was in his human form. I scratched behind his ear and he closed his eyes and made that same guttural sound that I had heard coming from his chest earlier. It was like a cat purring, but deep and more intense. His reaction to my touch made me bolder; I ran my hands down the length of his sleek body and down his long black tail. He pulled his tail out of my hands and turned over onto his back. I laughed and rubbed his belly. He flipped back over onto his stomach and stretched out laying his head back down in his massive paws. I stretched my body out to measure the size of the cat. He was pretty much the same size as Adriano in human form. He leaned into me and nuzzled me with his head.

"Okay, Adriano. I believe you." Instantly the feeling of soft black fur was gone and replaced by warm smooth flesh.

"So what are you thinking?" he asked as if nervous about my reaction. I leaned closer to him and wrapped my arms around his neck.

"I think that is the coolest thing I have ever seen." I grabbed his lower lip with my mouth and sucked gently before releasing his mouth from my kiss. "But you really should have told me all of this before you marked me? I mean what if I want to mate with some other jaguar man." I was joking, but his facial expression became very serious.

"You are mine. He can't have you now." He bit down on his lower lip as soon as he said it and averted his eyes. I knew he had said something that he had not meant to say.

"Who can't have me now?" I asked trying to get him to give away more about his slip in words.

"Whatever other man you're referring to." He locked his mouth down on mine and kissed me urgently. I had the sense that he was doing it more to end the conversation that out of passion, but the longer the kiss went on, the more passionate and exploratory it became. I'm sure he knew exactly how many fillings I had.

"Just promise me one thing," I asked breathlessly between kisses.

"Anything, Gatinho."

"If you feel the need to bite me again, please do it in a softer place so it won't hurt so much."

"I'm sorry, it needed to be somewhere on your body that would be easily visible. From now on when I bite you, it will be more intimate." He brushed his fingers across my lower lip. "Just little love bites."

I laid back down waiting for him to continue our passionate kisses and consummate our marriage, but he simply lay next to me and told me to sleep. I didn't argue or pursue any more physical contact because I was still shocked by what he could do and I did not want to move any further into the relationship physically until I had time to think.

I could not guess why he didn't try to seduce me further. Maybe he sensed my apprehension or maybe he had other plans entirely.

The Honeymoon is Over

We spent the rest of our vacation slash honeymoon, getting to know each other better, which was good since I was now married to a supernatural creature. He told me about his abilities, about how fast he could run, and how when he was home in the rainforest, he enjoyed being in his jaguar form. He had an acute sense of smell and hearing. His whiskers gave him lots of information about what was going on around him. He said it was like having an internal GPS system. He tried not to feed in is jaguar form because he found it made him more aggressive. I could sense that there was more he was leaving out. When I asked him why he chose me instead of a woman with his abilities, he explained that he just felt that we were supposed to be together. He said he had felt it since that first night we had met in the bar. I did not discuss my abilities with him. In fact, I was not sure if I still had them. I still had not decoded the dream about the baby. Maybe Adriano's presence in my life was messing with my abilities or maybe there just was not anything to see, but anyway it seemed like small beans compared to everything that he could do. The physical transformation was just so impressive.

When we returned to Kentson, I wasn't sure where to go. My things were in the apartment I shared with Rhett. I had managed to ignore all his calls and texts, so I was not sure what he was doing. I had sent him, as well as, Poppy and Dixie a text message with a picture of Adriano and me getting married. The message read, *From Mr. and Mrs. Adriano Medeiros.* Dixie had replied with an *OMG* and *Call me ASAP.* I did not call her. I just did not want to hear anything about Rhett.

Adriano and I discussed what to do agreeing that I should go to the apartment alone to get my things. Adriano did not think that he could avoid ripping Rhett's throat out if he saw him touching me. He wanted to maintain his sanity and he told me that he was sure that he could trust me to come back to him. I reassured him that I would. There was this intense emotional and physical need that I felt to be with him and I was having way too much fun not to come back to him. I explained that we would have to do something about his apartment. It needed to be updated or at the least cleaned professionally.

Adriano parked my car in front of the garage where he had left his motorcycle. He kissed me and we made plans to meet back at his apartment. I slid over to the driver's side pulling into my usual parking place in front of my apartment. I let myself in and found the apartment empty. All that remained were four boxes of clothes and personal items sitting in the middle of the living room. Rhett had taken everything else. I couldn't blame him. There was a handwritten note on top of one of the boxes. It simply read:

"I hope you are happy and that we can still be friends. Love, Rhett." I began to cry and for the first time I mourned the end of my relationship with Rhett. It was the end of a great friendship. I think that is what made me more upset than anything else.

I lost my best friend. I failed him. Didn't he deserve a change at happiness and if Poppy was the girl to do that for him then I should have seen it long ago. I hadn't given him a fair chance to explain his actions. For all I knew he thought that I was cheating on him because of the flowers that Adriano had sent me. I stayed in the living room and lay next to the boxes staring at the ceiling fan as it turned. Then I worked up the courage to move on. I placed each box into my car and drove to Adriano's apartment—our apartment. He was standing outside in the parking lot waiting for me.

"I was worried about you. What took so long?" he asked as he hugged me tight to his chest. I tried to hide my tear stained face from him, but I know that he saw.

"Sorry, I just sat there to think for a little while. Rhett moved out already. There were only a few boxes with my things in them. They're in my car." I turned to open the trunk and grab a box.

"Don't worry about that now." He pulled me back to him. "We have to go to Brazil. My mother is sick. I need to see her before she dies." He went on to explain that his sister had called and left a message on the answering machine in his apartment. He tried to call home, but no one answered. We jumped in the car; it contained our luggage from our trip to Las Vegas. It would have to be good enough for now. I phoned Claire and told her that I wouldn't be returning to the office for another week. I asked her to call around and find someone who could fill in for me for the next week. She agreed and expressed concern over what was going on and why had I eloped with a complete stranger instead of Dr. Foret. I told her not to worry that my new husband was taking me to meet his family in Brazil and that I would call her as soon as I knew when I was coming home.

When we reached Brazil, there was a limousine waiting for us outside the airport. I stood gawking at the long shiny black car as the driver got out and opened the door for us. Adriano grabbed my hand and pulled me inside the plush interior.

"You got some 'splaining to do, Lucy." I said, as I watched Adriano open two bottles of expensive European mineral water in the super fancy glass bottles.

"Gatinho, you're in Brazil. Ricky Ricardo was Cuban." He handed me one of the bottles, shaking his head. I took a sip then placed it into one of the cup holders near me. I crossed my arms and sighed. He leaned in and kissed my neck and then pulled my white t-shirt down my arm so he could brush his mark on my shoulder with his lips. This mark held more significance than he was letting on.

"I love you," he whispered and then moved his hands into my hair to turn my face to his. "Do you love me?" He asked before kissing me passionately. *How does he expect me to answer when I can barely breathe?*

He pulled away from the long languorous kiss and rubbed his nose across the edge of my jaw.

"I barely know you," I answered once my breathing returned to normal.

"Can't you feel it, Gatinho? Can't you feel this thing between us?" He pushed my hair behind my ear and kissed my shoulder. "I want to hear you say you love me."

"I'm just not sure I'm there yet," I said honestly. I knew I did not love him. I did have some feelings for him, but they were strange feelings. It was like someone else's emotions were filling me. I could not shake it. The feelings were warm and loving one minute, then angry the next. My brain was inhabited by a level of fuzziness that until now I had attributed to all the Vegas nightlife and alcohol we had been consuming. I shook my head maybe it was all the flying we had been doing. Could it just be an extreme case of overindulgence in alcohol and jet lag?

Adriano did not reply to my uncertain answer. He pouted at first, and then he placed his hand over my mouth so that the soft fleshy junction between his thumb and forefinger were between my teeth. He was going to bite me and didn't want me to make a sound. I felt him lift my shirt and bite down on the exposed part of my breast. I was getting used to the bites. The act of the bite was sensual and intimate just as he had described. For some unexplainable reason, I actually began to look forward to them. They healed quickly. He said it had something to do with the antibacterial properties of his saliva. The first bite on my shoulder was bigger and was inflicted in a way to make sure that it would leave a permanent scar. None of the smaller softer bites had left scars. After each bite he spent time licking and kissing the area to make sure it healed. It was a slow pleasurable torture that each time I thought would finally break my resolve not to sleep with him until I was really ready.

The most unusual thing was that neither of us had taken our relationship further than kissing and the biting. He seemed almost scared to take it further than an occasional show of affection. This only added to my confusion after he had been so forward with me in my apartment. In Vegas I told him that I wanted to slow things down sexually, saying that I wanted to take things slower now that I was sober and he seemed to be okay with giving me some time.

When we pulled up to the estate, my mouth dropped open again. The house was backed by lush rainforest and was surrounded by tall tropical plants and flowers on all sides. It was beautiful—actually breathtaking. It was nothing like the shabby simple homes in my great grandmother's village.

I was intimidated by the sheer size of the house. It would be better to describe it as a plantation. Adriano pulled me to him and kissed me once more before we turned to go through the large wrought iron gate. In the center of each gate was a large letter B with two large jaguars fighting around it.

"Remember, no matter what happens once we're inside, I'm your husband and I will protect you. Don't let anyone scare you." I nodded and slid my hand into his.

He must be kidding, right. Of course, I was nervous; he was leading me into a mansion full of half human half jaguar people. These were creatures that I had no idea that even existed. They are going to hate me; I was the older woman who married their baby boy. I started to giggle and could not stop. Maybe it was my nervousness or maybe just the total absurdity of the whole situation.

"What's so funny?" he asked, as he opened the gate.

"I just realized I'm a cougar married to a jaguar."

"Good grief." He shook his head and walked us through the

front door. "You're delirious, Gatinho."

We were greeted by a servant who welcomed and directed us to the dining room where his family was having their evening meal. I felt really self-conscious about the way we were dressed. I would have preferred to clean up and change before meeting everyone. Adriano was anxious to introduce me to his family. He reassured me that I looked beautiful and didn't smell too bad. He laughed when he said this so I think he might be teasing me.

The men stood when we entered the room. There were three men and each left the table and extended their hand to Adriano. He shook each man's hand in turn. The first man was older and must have been his father. The second man looked older than Adriano but not quite my age. He was shorter than the other men and built round at the middle. He was definitely not a blood relative. The third man … well let's just say I would have recognized him anywhere.

They were the same height. His black hair was cut short and his eyes were copper just like Adriano's. The blood red birthmark covering the right side of his face was slightly larger than I remembered. *How didn't I see this coming? Of course —they were brothers.* He was dressed in a white and blue striped polo shirt and khaki slacks. He was not quite as muscular as I remembered. He probably spent less time worrying about his body than his younger brother did. Don't get me wrong, from the look of his roped forearms, he was still in great shape, but I could tell that over the years other things had become more important to him.

Just looking at him again caused my stomach to flip and my body to tingle the way it used to. He was the only man who could ever make me feel that way. Adriano wrapped his arm around my waist. He could probably sense the change in my body. Over the past week I learned that he could sense the slightest change in my mood or my body. He explained that it was because of his heightened senses.

"Hello, Marco. It's been a long time," I mustered up the courage to say. I wanted to jump into his arms and kiss him, but Adriano's strong arm held me firmly in place.

"Biddy, is it really you?" The corner of his mouth twitched up into a sad smile.

"You recognize me?" I looked around for evidence of a wife or a girlfriend. There was none.

"It's hard to forget someone like you." I thought about what this meant. Marco must have the same abilities as Adriano. He was just as handsome as I remembered. I did not need my psychic talents to recognize him. His features, especially his smile, had been burned into my heart.

"Yes, isn't she breathtaking?" Adriano said, kissing my cheek before looking back at his brother. "Everyone, I'd like you to meet my beautiful wife, Biddy." Everyone except Marco cheered in congratulations. The women got up from the table and ran over to embrace us. Once the hugs and kisses were over, everyone sat back down at their seats.

Two more place settings had been added during all the excitement. Adriano and I joined the group. He leaned into me and went around the table to tell me who each person was. The older man at the head of the table was his father, Leonardo. His older sister, Carolina, was sitting next to his father. She was petite and very slim. She had long straight black hair and the same copper eyes as her brothers. Carolina's husband, Ignacio, the short round man was sitting next to her. Adriano's twin sister, Adriana, sat near Marco. Marco watched us as Adriano talked intimately in my ear. I could feel Marco's eyes on me following my every move.

I managed to make it through dinner without freaking out, but none of this made sense. Adriano owed me a big explanation. I had lots of questions for him, like why he lied about his last name. I guess that answer was pretty obvious. He knew I would recognize the name. I guess the real question was why had he married me?

Adriano led me to a room with a large antique mahogany four poster bed with mosquito netting draped from the wooden rod between each post. Across from the bed, a large set of French doors opened out onto a balcony that overlooked a back yard which was filled with palms and other prehistorically large tropical plants.

I chose to lie on the hammock on the balcony trying to fig-ure out exactly how to find out what it was I wanted to know. I had no clue what was going on.

Adriano joined me on the balcony cuddling up next to me on the hammock. He had stripped down to his jeans. I just laid there next to him—fuming in silence.

"Go ahead, Gatinho. I know you're upset with me. What do you want to know?"

"Yes, I am upset with you. I don't even know where to start." He kissed me tenderly and moved to nuzzle my neck. "Why did you marry me? For goodness sakes what is our last name?"

He raised his head to look into my eyes. "First of all, I want you to know that I do love you. Like I've told you all along, you are mine. I don't intend on letting you go." He paused for me to digest what he was saying. "Originally, I tracked you down for one reason. Pure revenge. I hate my brother and he loves you. What better way to hurt him than to make sure that he could never touch you again?" It was more of a statement than a question. He pushed down the small strap of my nightgown to expose my shoulder and gently rubbed his mark with his thumb. I remembered the day he gave me the mark and how he explained that no other man of his kind would dare mate with a women who was marked by another jaguar shifter. "Your name is whatever you want it to be. My full name is Adriano Leonardo Medeiros Barnardos."

"What if I want him instead of you?" I asked out of more than curiosity.

"The only way that can happen is if I die. I'm stronger and faster than he is; he would never be able to accomplish it." He pouted. "Why would you want him when you have me?"

That question had the simplest and truest of answers—love. I still loved Marco. I had never stopped loving him. My feelings for him were like an eternal flame that no amount of time could ever douse. No about of animal magnetism or perfect abs could change that. Seeing Marco again made me realize that he was the reason I did not want to marry Rhett. I knew in my heart I still wanted to be with Marco. He would always be the only man that I would ever want to spend my life with.

Adriano kissed the inside of my neck and this intense feeling of need enveloped me. It was so powerful, unlike anything that

I Married the ~~Bartender, a Mythical Creature,~~ the Wrong Man!

I had felt before. It was not entirely sexual. There were some other emotions mixed in with it. They were not my own feelings and I just could not explain them.

Adriano's warm mouth moved over my exposed collarbone. "I love you," he breathed over my skin, which sent a chill up my spine. He moved to position himself on top of me; he wanted to make love, which was clear.

"Not tonight. I'm not ready," I said with a scolding tone. "I'm still angry and I don't even know if I ..."

"I know, Gatinho. Let me make love to you. It will make us both feel better," he interrupted me before I could say that I did not want to be married to him.

He pressed his body to mine and resumed kissing me softly in the crook of my neck.

"I said no!" I stood suddenly and the hammock flipped Adriano out onto the floor. He landed on all fours and fazed into his jaguar form. He roared and barred his teeth. His muzzle wrinkling upward in anger; he looked as if he might attack. I stood still and silent as he stared at me like some kind of prey. He slowly stepped towards me one massive paw at a time; rubbing the length of his body along my bare legs. He leaned into the rub in that slow seduction that cats are famous for. I dropped my hand as he passed around me circling one more time and I rubbed his soft fur from the top of his head down his back. He jumped to the top of the stone balcony railing and then into a nearby tree.

The balcony was covered in torn and tattered pieces of his blue jeans. They did not survive his fazing. I turned to the bedroom

and decided to just go to sleep. I was tired and I definitely did not feel like playing his games tonight. *How did he expect me to react?* I fell asleep with this question on my mind.

His whiskers tickled me as he rubbed his face along mine. In the short time that I had known him, I was used to Adriano's need to nuzzle me in his jaguar form. I almost felt sorry for him because of him choosing me to be his wife he couldn't mate with me in his cat form, something that would be normal if he had chosen a woman who could shift. It made me feel inadequate as his mate and as a mate for Marco for that matter. Maybe that was also one of the reasons I had refused to make love to him.

I sat up in the bed and stared at him. He rested his large head in my lap as I stroked his head and ears. He produced a beautiful low purring sound. I rubbed the underneath of his chin as he gazed up at me. There was a pain in his glowing copper eyes. Without question, I knew that the source of pain in those eyes was me.

"Come to bed. Hold me," I offered. The large black cat made a groaning sound and lowered his head. He turned and ran back out the doors and off the balcony.

Okay, so he must still be angry that I refused him earlier. I rolled over and went back to sleep. All of this traveling had worn me out.

When I awoke, I felt Adriano's warm body pressed against mine and his heavy arms wrapped around me tightly. So, apparently he was not mad at me anymore and to be honest, I didn't know how I felt about him. I was angry with him for tricking me, but he did something to me that I still couldn't explain. It was hard to maintain my anger towards him as his body felt so good next to mine.

"Are you still angry, Gatinho?" he asked in a whisper as he nuzzled my ear.

"Maybe," I smiled. I knew he could not see my face since he was behind me, but he could probably tell by the tone of my voice. My tone felt lighter and definitely more playful. There was something about the way he had come to me in his cat form with those sad eyes that lessened my anger.

"I've brought you a present. I hope it will soften your anger and maybe help you to forgive me." He pulled back my hair and kissed my neck.

"What kind of present?" I liked surprises.

"I visited my mother last night. She wants to meet you. The present is really from her. I told her that you were angry with me. She assured me that once I gave you this you would immediately forgive me for whatever I had done wrong."

"Did you tell her that you tricked me into marrying you to take revenge on your only brother?" My tone turning harder as the words escaped my lips.

"Well, no, and when you put it that way, huh…" he sighed. "I'll just give it back to her and tell her you didn't want it."

"I would like to see it." I could not resist at least knowing what it was.

Adriano laughed and slid my wedding ring off of my finger and back onto his hand where it had been before our wedding. It was then that I remembered that Marco had worn a similar ring so many years ago. He replaced it with a large square diamond. The ring Rhett had given me was over two carrots and this ring was four times the size of that diamond. I had never seen such a magnificent stone.

"Oh, Adriano! It's beautiful." I held it up to the light coming in from outside and the ring sparkled.

"So does that mean you forgive me?" he asked hopefully as he planted a kiss on top of my head.

"No." I swallowed a lump in my throat. "I have a few questions."

"Okay." He twirled the ring around on my finger admiring it from all angles.

"You say that you love me, but if you really truly love me, then you wouldn't have tricked me."

"That's more of a statement than a question," he stated flatly.

"Adriano, please explain it to me again."

"I admit that I messed up. I shouldn't have brought you here. We should have stayed in the U.S. and you would never have known he was my brother, but I needed to see my mother and I just couldn't resist hurting Marco. Admit that before you saw him that you were falling in love with me."

I turned and looked into his eyes. He was vulnerable and so much like a little boy. He was telling me the truth and he was right. I had been falling in love with him. He had swept me off my feet. When I looked at him, I just wanted to take care of him and protect him.

"I do love you, Adriano, but there are all kinds of love." What I felt for him was not nearly as strong as my bond to Marco. "You have to promise me you'll tell me the truth from now on."

He nodded. Before he could say anything, I kissed him— long and hard. I had willingly married him to hurt Rhett. Did I really have a right to judge what he did? The answer was simple. No. We deserved each other. He returned my kiss and intensified the passionate expression by ripping my nightgown in half. The act of it was shocking but exciting. No man had ever ripped any article of clothing off of me before. He looked at me and I could feel an intense hunger and need. I wasn't sure if it was mine or his.

"Are you ready to make love now?" he asked. Before I could answer him, my stomach growled; that loud embarrassing grumble that always seems to happen at the most inopportune times.

"We have to get you fed. I want you to keep up your strength." He laughed as he handed me a dress from the closet. It was a white cotton sundress with small spaghetti straps. "Put this one on. My mother will like it."

"Can I meet her now?" I asked as I pulled the dress over my head. "I want to thank her for the ring." I eyed it approvingly making it sparking in the ray of the morning sun across the light wood floor.

Adriano nodded is assent to my request. He was pleased that I wanted to meet his mother. It was easy to see that he loved her very much. I suppose it isn't unusual for a baby boy to love his mother that way. She must have adored him and spoiled him when she could.

He wrapped my hand in his and led me out of the room down the stairs into the dining room. It was close to lunch time now so no one else was in the room. He sat me at the table and told me to stay there while he found us something for breakfast. I looked around the room admiring the dark heavy wood furnishings and the colorful art on the walls. Adriano emerged from the side door with a plate full of various kinds of fruit, cheeses, and crackers. He lifted a piece of ripe yellow mango to my lips and the juice dripped down my chin. He leaned in and licked the juice that was dripping down my neck.

"Sweet." He smiled as he lifted another piece of fruit to my lips.

"It is delicious." I opened my mouth to take in the next slice of mango.

"Yeah, the fruit is good, too." We both giggled. From the outside looking in I imagined we looked like the perfect newly-wed couple. He gazed at me adoringly and I flirted and maintained constant contact with him. There was just something that told me to act this way even though intellectually I knew it was wrong and I should run back to Rhett. Rhett was safe compared to the men in this house. I just couldn't overcome the power that Adriano had over me. He had me wanting more but was that wanting enough to overcome those older deep rooted feelings I had been trying to push down all these years for his older brother.

We finished off the plate of food and found our way back upstairs. Adriano stopped in front of his mother's bedroom door and knocked. His knuckles barely hit the surface of the door. I fidgeted as we waited to be allowed inside.

"Calm down, Gatinho." He hugged me tightly. "She's going to love you."

A short older woman opened the door and Adriano lead me inside the dark room. The bed in the middle of the huge room was similar to the bed that Adriano and I had shared the night before. The woman sitting in the middle of the bed had long black hair that fell across her shoulder. Her eyes were closed but I did not think that she was asleep. Her breathing was ragged. She was an older version her daughters. She must have been in her early sixties. Adriano sat on the edge of his mother's bed and touched her hand gently.

"Mãe." He waited for her to open her eyes. "There is someone I'd like you to meet." She turned to look at me. Her eyes were the same shade of copper as the rest of her family. "This is my wife, Biddy." He stretched out his free hand and motioned me closer.

"Hello, it's a pleasure to meet you." I lifted my hand and placed it on Adriano's shoulder. "Adriano and I would like to thank you for the beautiful gift. I will wear it proudly." What was I saying? I did not want to wear his ring. I did not want to be married

to him. Who was controlling my thoughts because it certainly was not me? I did not want to hurt him, but I did not love him the way I loved Marco.

"You're welcome. He told me he didn't give you a proper ring when you were married. Of course, I would have preferred if you would have been married here, but I understand that it was a spontaneous decision. Young love can be so impetuous." She lifted herself up onto her elbows to adjust her body. Adriano stood to help her. He fluffed her pillows and bent to gently kiss her forehead. "She's beautiful; take good care of her," the woman whispered to her son just loud enough for me to hear.

"She's tired. We can come back another time and visit her. Let's go for a walk in the garden," Adriano whispered after tucking the blanket around his mother's frail body.

We apologized for interrupting her morning nap and Adriano lead me down the stairs and through the house. He explained that his mother was suffering from ovarian cancer that had spread to her uterus and liver. Her physicians wanted to perform a hysterectomy to remove the female organs and try to remove the tumors in the liver, but his mother refused. They were all basically just waiting for her to die. I tried to console him, but it was obvious that he wished she would fight harder.

In the family room over the massive marble mantled fireplace there was a family portrait in a gilded frame. I could identify all of the family members except for the little girl sitting in Marco's lap. There was something familiar about the little girl. Unlike the rest of the family, her hair was light brown and her eyes were blue. She did not look like the rest of them.

"Who is that little girl?" I pointed to the picture as we walked out to the garden. My dream was beginning to make sense and the little girl had brown hair and blue eyes like the baby in my dream. The silver rattle with the feline symbol also made sense. The baby had been raised by the family of jaguar people.

"That is my adorable niece Elena." He picked a beautiful purple orchard and placed it in my hair behind my ear. "Marco's daughter."

"Marco's daughter?" I asked puzzled. "I thought you said your brother had never married."

"He never married. He adopted her when she was an infant. I was still a child when she came to live with us."

"Why wasn't she at dinner last night?" I asked as I adjusted the flower in behind my ear.

"She was probably with her friends," he explained. We sat on a concrete bench in the middle of the lush garden. "I'm sure she'll be here tonight. Marco keeps close tabs on her. He is very protective. The poor girl isn't allowed to date yet. She's sixteen. It's got to be hard for her to deal with her overprotective father without the love and guidance of a mother."

"Hmmm." I sat with my head in my hands. I needed to talk to Marco. I needed to know more about Elena. We spent the rest of the afternoon walking around the estate. Adriano led me through every square inch of the enchanting gardens. The air was humid but the lush foliage and large variety of flowers provided a perfume to it that made it more than bearable.

The family gathered in the dining room. Tonight I was more prepared to see Marco and hopefully meet Elena. Adriano and I were dressed more appropriately this time. He was wearing tan slacks and a nice blue oxford shirt. I had selected a pretty red blouse and black skirt. We were placed in the same seating arrangements as the night before.

Marco and Elena entered the dining room after everyone else was already inside. I could not understand what they were arguing about, but it was obvious that they were upset with each other. I remembered being her age; it was difficult being a teenage girl, especially one with my abilities. When Elena fully entered into the room, my jaw dropped open, and I gasped in awe.

"Marco, may I speak to you in private?" Everyone turned to look at me. They must have been shocked by my commanding tone. I stared at the young girl while I waited for him to answer. My fears were confirmed. Elena was our daughter. He had raised her without me. Her hair and eyes were identical to mine. Her skin was darker than mine, but she probably spent more time in the sun than I did. Looking at her was like looking back in time.

"What's going on?" Elena said as she stared back and forth between Marco and me.

"This is your new Aunt Biddy," Adriano wrongly explained. *Should I correct him?*

"Hello, Elena. I'm happy to meet you." I did not know if I wanted to correct Adriano. I wanted to tell her that I wasn't her aunt, but her mother. I needed to speak to Marco. We needed to straighten a few things out.

"Are you pulling my leg? She's old enough to be your mother, Uncle Adriano." Elena frowned.

Everyone except Adriano chuckled at the young girl. I had to admit it was pretty funny. I liked her sense of humor.

"No, Elena. She is only six years older than me." Adriano corrected.

"Elena, would you excuse your father and I so we can have a little chat." I turned to leave the room. Adriano stood to follow me.

"No! You stay here. This is between Marco and me," I insisted.

"But Gatinho, I think I have a right to know why you are so upset."

"I'll explain later. Please stay here." Adriano nodded in agreement. He didn't like it, but he seemed to know better than to question me further.

I turned to Marco and pointed my index finger in his direction. "You, out there, NOW!"

He sighed and stood to follow me out of the room. We walked across the hall into a room that served as Marco's office. It was furnished in heavy masculine furniture and large wooden bookshelves. He sat on the edge of his desk facing me.

"What…how…why," I began but was so flabbergasted that

there did not seem like a good way to start the conversation.

"Biddy, I felt the same way when I saw you yesterday."

"I don't even have to ask you if that is our daughter. She looks exactly like I did at that age."

"Yes, I know. It's amazing how much she looks like you. She's just as beautiful as her mother." He looked at me tenderly caressing my face with his eyes. Oh, those damn eyes! I felt my resolve to be angry melting under his gaze. I picked up a small black jaguar porcelain figurine from the side table nearest me and through it at him. It shattered against his desk leaving a gash in the beautiful dark wood.

He didn't even flinch.

"Feel better now?" he asked. "I have other valuable antiques that you can smash if you feel the need."

"No, I'm fine now," I said rubbing my forehead with my hand. "But, how did she end up with you? I never told you I was pregnant."

"After a few months of being apart, I missed you. I went to find you and I saw that you were pregnant. I did some investigating and found out that you had put off college because of the baby and that you planned on giving the baby up for adoption. It seemed impossible, but I managed to adopt her. I was glad that you asked for a closed adoption. There was no way for you to find out what I had done. I decided to raise our daughter and let you go, so you could have a normal life. I was sure you would marry a nice normal man. How did you end up with my evil little brother?"

"Don't change the subject." The truth was I still did not know why they hated each other, but that was the least of my problems.

"Look, if you would have married me seventeen years ago we wouldn't be going through any of this and I would know my own daughter." I burst into tears. He wrapped his arms around me like we had never been apart.

"I wanted you to have a normal life. You had no clue what you were asking when you begged to stay with me." He pushed my hair behind my ears.

"I was pregnant and scared, Marco. I loved you. I just wanted to be with you. Nothing else mattered to me." I wrapped my hands into his shirt, pulling him even closer to me. The heat of his body was so familiar and comforting.

"Why didn't you tell me you were pregnant?" he asked.

"I was going to tell you, but you were so cruel trying to get me to leave. I just didn't know what to do." He had been intentionally brutal; telling me that he did not want me and that he had only used me for my body. He had said that he was tired of me and wanted someone new.

"Okay, we've established that I'm the bad guy here. It's my turn to ask you a question."

I nodded in agreement and wiped away the tears from my eyes.

"Did you know he was my brother when you married him?"

"No, he didn't tell me. He said his last name was Medeiros. I had no idea until I saw you yesterday. I think the element of surprise was the whole point. When I looked into his eyes, they reminded me of you, but I didn't really think you would be related."

"Medeiros is our mother's maiden name. Did he tell you about us?" he asked.

"Yes, he said he wanted to hurt you. He wanted to make sure you could never have me again. He said that you still…" I trailed off the last words not wanting to be the one to finish the statement. I wanted to hear him say it.

"Love you," He finished my sentence and stared into my eyes. "Yes, he is right. I've never stopped loving you."

"I've never stopped loving you, Marco. Please forgive me for marrying him. I was drunk." Of course, my drunkenness was not the only reason, but the reason did not really seem all that important.

"It's not your fault. He tricked you, but…" he pulled me away to look straight into my eyes. "Did he tell you about what we can do?"

I nodded. "Told me, showed me. Why didn't you tell me? You knew about my abilities." It hurt that I had trusted him totally with my deepest secrets, but he had not felt comfortable enough to trust me with his own.

"I didn't want to scare you." He walked toward the large fireplace and leaned against the mantle. "Has he marked you?" I unbuttoned the top two buttons on my blouse and lowered the left side to show him the large scar. He cringed at the sight of it.

"Is that the only one?" he asked as he rubbed his temples. All of this must be giving him a headache.

"No, he bites me every day. That's the extent of our physical contact." I wanted him to know that I had not had sex with his brother.

"You mean you two haven't consummated the marriage?" He smiled.

"No, I told you we got married while I was drunk then he bit me and it scared the crap out of me at first. I've told him I'm not ready to take the relationship to the next level."

"Good girl," he said proudly.

"Why does he keep biting me?" I asked. I knew it had more significance than Adriano was letting on.

"He's doing that to keep you interested. Our saliva has a chemical in it that causes our mates to be more physically and sexually attracted to us. If he does it often enough you'll actually be able to feel what he's feeling. Your emotions will be connected. It's very powerful."

"That explains why my head feels fuzzy. I keep feeling emotions that aren't mine. Like right now, I am feeling worried and angry, but they don't feel like my feelings."

"You're natural abilities may help you combat the power of the bites, but you will have to work at it," he added.

"You and I never needed magical saliva." We both laughed. "It still doesn't explain the connection I felt to him before he bit me. We were like magnets being pulled together by some unseen force."

"He is handsome, like his older brother. It could just be good old fashioned lust." His eye lids dropped slightly. His head was hurting I could tell. I put my hands on both sides of his head and concentrated on his pain. I did not want to think about the lust that I was feeling for Adriano and I especially did not want Marco thinking about it. I spoke the ritual prayer for healing with my eyes closed because I could not concentrate on my energy if we were staring at each other. I felt his body uncoil in relief when his head stopped throbbing and I lowered my hands.

"Thank you," he took my hands in his and kissed the palms of each one.

"About Elena, should we tell her that I'm her mother?" I asked, hoping for his agreement. I wanted a relationship with her. I missed so much of her life and I did not want to miss one more moment.

"Is that what you want?" he asked.

"Yes. Maybe. I don't know. I want to do what's best for her." Of course that is what I want. I want to know my daughter. "You know her better than I do, how will she react?"

"She's just like you. She and I are fighting about boys. She could really use her mother right now. Think about it and let me know when you're ready. We'll tell her together."

"One more question. Why didn't you allow some nice young childless couple to adopt her?" I was curious as to why a young and apparently rich boy would give up his youth to raise a child.

"I couldn't take the chance of her being able to shift. I had to protect my people's secrets." He looked down at his shoes and then slowly back up to my eyes. "And I thought if she was with me, it would make being separated from my true love easier to bear."

"I assumed you had to have the gene from both parents to shift." My body tingled as he referred to me as his true love. It amazed me that after so many years the man could still melt me that way.

Marco went on to explain that he had suspicions when he met me that I carried the genetic traits of his people. My eyes he said contained tiny copper flecks. He spent a lot of time gazing into my eyes back then. He knew them better than I did.

The reason for my visits to Brazil had been to see my Noni. She was a Brazilian native who practiced Umbanda. Her position was as a priestess. Her people called her Mae-de-Santo. Her advice and healing abilities were widely sought after. She taught me not to be afraid of my abilities or the spirits who visited me. However, she never told me about the jaguars. Marco continued to explain that only those with the gift discussed it amongst one another.

"Elena does not have the ability. She has no idea about the rest of us," he said. So she is unaware of what her father's family can do. He has managed to keep it from her all her life.

"Elena is just a normal teenage girl?" I asked. I knew her

birth had been normal so she would not have any of my abilities.

"Yes…very hormonal." We both chuckled.

"Thank you for taking care of her. I just couldn't do it alone. Giving her up was the hardest thing I ever had to do. It was like giving her and you up all over again. It nearly killed me." He pulled my face up to look into his eyes. The emotion on his face was clear. Desire. He lowered his lips to mine without actually touching them.

"His mark doesn't mean we can't be together. It just means that if I make love to you, he has a right to challenge me in our jaguar forms. He'll have the right to kill me."

"He told me the only way I could have you was if he were dead." I cringed at the thought of losing Marco again.

"That would probably be the easiest way, but he knows I wouldn't do that as long as my mother is still alive."

"He said you wouldn't be able to kill him. He said he's stronger and faster than you." Marco smiled and lowered his lips fully onto mine. The soft brush of his lips made my stomach flip and my body ache. It was long overdue. My lips had been waiting for his for the last sixteen years.

He made a low guttural sound deep in his throat, and I realized that it was him in my room last night. Marco was the cat that did not stay when I spoke.

"He is definitely all those things, but I'm smarter. I'll find a way for us to be together as a family," he said, reassuringly.

I nodded as he released me. We both straightened out our

clothes.

"Try to discourage his biting without raising his suspicions. I need you to be able to think clearly."

"Marco, no matter what you see between Adriano and me. Please know that I never stopped loving you, but this hold he has on me is powerful. Sometimes I can't help my reaction." I knew that he understood this better than I did, but I imagine it would hurt him to see Adriano and me in any intimate situation.

We rejoined the family and casually entered into the dinner conversations that were already underway. Adriano was tense. His anger was palpable. He looked back and forth between Marco and me for some clue as to what we had been discussing.

"Aunt Biddy," Elena began, "since you seem to know my Papa, would you please tell him that a girl my age should be allowed to date?" she said pointing to Marco with her dinner fork.

I wiped the corner of my mouth with the white linen napkin and smiled.

"Elena, I would be happy to discuss it with your Papa, but I feel like I should get to know you better first. But in general, I think a beautiful sixteen year old girl should be allowed to go on a date."

Elena smiled, "Oh, thank you, Aunt Biddy, I would like to get to know you better too."

"How about tomorrow? Can we go shopping?" I turned to Marco. "If that's alright with you … Papa?"

He smiled and nodded. His expression looked appreciative that I was trying to take this slowly.

"But, Gatinho," Adriano interrupted. "I have special plans for us tomorrow."

I turned to face him and sweetly asked, "Can I please spend the day with Elena?" I leaned in closer to whisper in his ear. "I promise I'll make it up to you." This chemical mating thing was strong. Even though I loved Marco, I still wanted to please Adriano. He nodded in agreement, but I could tell he was still upset.

Elena and I made plans to meet after breakfast. When supper was over Adriano and I went for a walk again through the garden. He was quiet, and when I did ask questions, he replied with sharp unfriendly answers.

"Would you feel better if you phased and went for a run?" I asked. "You seem like you need to work off some steam."

"I would feel better if my wife would tell me what was going on at dinner and why my brother's scent is all over her." He sniffed my neck and wrinkled his nose in distaste.

"First of all, his scent is on me because he held me while I cried." Adriano stopped in his tracks and placed his hands on the tops of my arms. I conveniently let off the part about Marco kissing me.

"Did he make you cry?"

"No, this whole situation is overwhelming and there is something else I need to discuss with you. But first I need your word that you will not repeat what I'm about to tell you to anyone, especially Elena."

"I promise." I looked around to make sure we were alone. It was obvious that I was apprehensive about speaking in the open. "No one is within hearing range," he reassured me.

"Good," I sighed. "Elena is my daughter."

Adriano stood in silence for a moment. "I know."

"But this morning you didn't tell me…"

"It wasn't for me to tell," he explained simply.

"I just don't understand you. Why are you doing this to me?" I swung my fist to hit him in the chest but instead he reached out and stopped it before it reached him catching my fist in the palm of his hand.

"Because I want to have a child with you. One that will have both our abilities." He bit down on his lower lip the minute the thought escaped his lips.

"What do you know about my abilities?" He looked at me and then down at the stone-paved pathway under our feet. I wrapped my hands in his shirt and pulled him closer. "Answer me!"

"See that's the thing. You don't even remember do you?" He shook his head in disappointment. I literally felt his disappointment mingled with sadness and anger. It slowly filled me until it was overwhelming and I almost choked on it. The feeling was so strong I felt has if a heavy object were pushing against my chest. It was suffocating in its intensity. "You are the center of my most memorable childhood experiences and you don't even remember me." I remained silent to his pain and waited for him to continue. "When I was little, I used to follow Marco out to the village where he would meet you. I watched him kissing you and touching you. Gatinho, you were the most beautiful girl I had ever seen. That is how I knew she was your daughter. She looks just like you did back then." He paused to catch his breath. "One day while I was watching you make love to him outside in the tall grass, I fell out of the tree that I was sitting in."

"You were watching us?" I asked in disbelief and horror. I never imagined anyone had been watching us make love. I felt my face prickling with embarrassment.

"I was in my Jaguar form, Marco had to know I was there, but he ignored me." He shrugged. "Anyway, when I fell, I fazed back to my human form and you heard me crying. You healed my leg."

"I remember, but Marco never told me you were his brother." Marco had insisted on carrying the boy home and we never spoke of it again. The experience of having a half naked woman healing your leg would be a memorable experience for anyone, especially a young boy.

"He didn't want you to meet any of us. He didn't want you to know what he was … to think he was a freak. When we got home, I told our father what you did and what I had seen the two of you doing. Father was angry at first, but then he tried to convince Marco to ask you to stay. He wanted him to marry you and I heard him talking about the possibility of the two of you being able to have a child who could have both of your abilities. My father did some checking into your family tree. Your great grandfather was a jaguar shifter and your great grandmother was an Umbanda High Priestess. She was very powerful."

We walked back towards the house as he continued to explain and I felt the intensity of his pain lighten. It was like him telling me about his past and his feelings were diminishing the weight of them. "My father saw the possibilities for our people if you were to give birth to a shifter who could heal others with his hands. Marco loved you too much to use you for our father's business interests."

"What do you mean?" I asked still not understanding why a jaguar healer would be so desirable.

"Father is what you would call a drug lord. A shifter with extra abilities would come in handy in his line of work. When one of his men is wounded fighting, they could be saved or healing could be offered to a village that is not cooperating in order to attain their allegiance." It sounded like they would intentionally hurt villagers and offer the healing as an incentive to their leaders for full cooperation in any illegal or immoral activity that was desired.

We walked in silence to our bedroom. I sat on the edge of the bed and took off my sandals. Adriano peeled off his shirt and joined me.

"So I guess Elena was a bit of a disappointment," I stated trying to understand this family.

"Only to my father," he smiled. "Marco was actually relieved when he realized she couldn't shift. Marco runs the legitimate side of our family business."

"Coffee." I interrupted remembering this from so many years ago. During the mornings, Marco would go to work and in the afternoons he would come to find me. He always smelled like coffee on those days. He was not in charge back then, but he was working with the laborers getting to know the business. He would bring Noni bags of coffee when he would come to find me. Like some kind of offering. "What part do you play in the family business?"

"None, yet," he said shaking his head in disgust. "I would like to inherit the entire operation, but father has always favored Marco. If I stay in the house, I get nothing as long as Marco is around or I…" He didn't finish the thought, but I had a pretty good idea of what angle he was working. I was Adriano's power play. He was going to use me to get what he wanted one way or another.

I found it hard to believe that Marco would want any part of the family's illegal business. It worried me that Elena grew up in a house where her grandfather ran such a business, but she seemed to be safe.

"So you wouldn't be happy working for your brother?" I asked.

"Never. Ever since the day you healed me, he has hated me, and I hate him. He blames me for telling father about you." He raised his hand and brushed the pads of his fingers down my cheek. I could feel his level of desire increasing in intensity. I looked down at his sculptured abdomen and felt my body giving in to that desire. My mind was going to have to be stronger than this. I just did not understand how I could be in love with one man and still want the body of another. There had to be something else going on.

He clouded my judgment for one thing. It was hard to think clearly when he had his hands on me like this.

"Gatinho, you are so beautiful." He leaned my back against the plush bed coverings. "I've wanted you to be mine since the moment you healed my leg. I've idolized you ever since that moment. I love you."

I couldn't bring myself to say it back to him. I may have been turned on by him, but I did not love him. Marco was right. Adriano and I had a serious case of lust and I was pretty sure there was something magical besides his aphrodisiac laden saliva. I kissed him to avoid him asking me to profess love to him. He was a hurt little boy deep down inside and I did not want to hurt him anymore. The tactic was effective at ending the conversation.

As he pulled his lips away from mine he stared intently into my eyes holding my gaze. I felt mesmerized like a small animal caught in the gaze of the hunter. It was powerful, a feeling of entrapment and excitement. I felt my heart rate increase as he unbuttoned my blouse. His fingers pushed back the fabric till the shirt slide over my shoulders and down my arms to the bed. He bent his head to lick and kiss his mark on my shoulder, his long hair tickled the skin on the back of my neck and I shivered.

"Does that feel good, Gatinho?" he asked smugly as he sat and watched me with those intense copper eyes.

"It's hard to imagine anything feeling much better." The comment slipped between my lips, but it was true. The feeling of his mouth on that mark was indescribable, but it was a bittersweet pleasure because I wanted that to be Marco's bite mark on my body.

He produced that familiar guttural noise deep in his chest that I was learning to associate with these jaguar men.

"Just imagine what it would feel like if you let me make love to you, Gatinho?" His mouth moved over the mark again, his tongue swirling over it. Then he trailed kisses down my neck.

"Ohh…" I said, between gasps of pleasure. "Please don't stop."

One corner of his mouth twitched as he tried to stop himself from smiling in self-satisfaction. It wasn't really me speaking. It was the mixture of the physical sensation of his mouth and tongue on that mark and the intensity of his emotions battling with my ability to reason. He lowered his head and continued to rain kisses down my body. I ran my fingers through his hair and I could feel the desire for him to bite me building inside of me. It was like I could feel what he was feeling; there was an intense sympathetic link between us that allowed me to feel his desires as my own. It was overwhelming how badly I wanted him to bite me again. I imagined this is what a drug addict feels like, needing that next fix.

"Where would you like to mark me next?" I asked my speech still not under my control. He looked up at me and smiled. He knew in this moment that he was winning. His plan was working. He lowered his gaze and then bit down on my inner thigh. The surge of pleasure and pain sated the craving I was having for his mark. The overwhelming feeling of calm and satisfaction that he felt as his teeth sank in to my leg and small amounts of my blood trickled into his mouth. *Oh, I'm in so much trouble.* I had to think of a way to fight against the overwhelming desire he was projecting into my mind through his emotions. I tried concentrating on other things … anything that could give me the strength to deny him again. I thought about Dixie. My sweet friend who was probably at home wondering what in the hell was wrong with me. If only she would reach out to me now. I mentally focused on her sending my need for her to check up on me. We had always had a close bond and I never kept anything from her. Well, except for my powers.

I heard something ringing. It sounded like it was coming from under the bed.

"My phone is ringing," I said.

"Let it ring," he grunted in between licks of the fresh wound.

"No, what if it's an emergency?" I asked. The phone continued to ring. I wrapped my fingers in his thick hair and pulled his head back, I pleaded with him with my eyes. He reached down and grabbed the phone from the floor.

The caller id revealed that it was Dixie. Thank goodness. This was just the break I needed. I would not have been able to hold him off any longer if she hadn't of called.

"Hey Dixie! I'm so glad you called."

Getting to know Elena

Elena and I met after breakfast just as we had planned. We spent the entire morning and early afternoon looking in and out of various stores. She enjoyed shopping. Her father apparently had a line of credit in many of the stores that allowed her to buy anything that she wanted. Elena told me he did not want her to date, but he spoiled her in every other imaginable way. From our conversations, I gathered that she was intelligent but overly sheltered. She told me about a boy that had asked her out and who she wanted to go out with. Her father refused. It was hard for me to give her much advice about the situation because I did not know Marco's reasons for not wanted her to date. I wondered if it was because he remembered how single minded boys her age can be. He certainly had been at that age. It had not taken him long to seduce me. I was weak willed when it came to saying no to him. I justified it at the time because I loved him so much and I just could not imagine how anything that felt so right could possibly be wrong.

"I think he is just concerned that you will have sex before you're really ready." I laid it out on the table.

"I've never even kissed a boy. Can we take it one step at a time, Aunt Biddy?"

"That's easy for you to say when you're here shopping with me, but believe me when your hormones take over and the guy is whispering in your ear how beautiful you are and how badly he wants you, he might even tell you that he loves you." I paused as we crossed the street. "It's easy to get lost in the passion of a moment like that."

"You sound like you've been there," she said, as she pointed towards a pretty dress in a store window.

"Yeah. I've been there, done that, got the T-shirt." *Unfortunately I'm still caught up in that situation.*

She giggled as we sat at an outdoor café to have lunch. "I just want to go on a date and maybe get a little good night kiss." She sighed.

"If you promise not to take it further than kissing, I think I might be able to talk your father into letting you go on a date," I said, before waving at a waiter to get his attention.

"Oh, thank you so much, Aunt Biddy." She hugged me tightly, and the smile on her face melted my heart. It made me aware of how much I had missed of seeing her grow up. I was jealous that Marco and even Adriano had gotten to spend so much time with her.

We ordered lunch and chatted about her interests and school work. She eventually returned the conversation to more a more interesting topic.

"Can I ask you a question?" she sipped her grape soda. I nodded in agreement. "If your Uncle Adriano's wife, how do you know my papa?"

"I met your papa a long time ago before I knew Adriano. We were friends."

"Just friends or were you more than friends?" She crunched

on a piece of ice from her drink. She reminded me so much of myself at her age.

"That's awfully forward of you to ask, young lady." I smiled. "But I guess you're old enough to understand. "Yes, your father and I dated."

"This is like a soap opera." Her eyes grew wide with innocent amazement.

"Yeah, you're right. It is just like a soap opera. A really awful soap opera," I added.

"So did you love him?" she asked. She seemed genuinely concerned. I could tell that she loved her father and her uncle. If I were her I would be worried that my new Aunt would cause problems between them.

"Yes, and he loved me, but it was a long time ago. When I met your uncle, I didn't know they were brothers," I explained. I did not want Elena thinking that I was some kind of vindictive women who was out to hurt her family.

"Papa still loves you." She swirled her fingertip on the rim of her glass as she looked at me out of the corner of her blue eyes. "I can tell by the way he looks at you. I've seen him date other women. He's never looked at any of them the way he looks at you." We both smiled. She was perceptive.

"Life is so complicated, Elena." I watched my daughter as she daintily sipped her soda and nibbled at the food on her plate. "What do you know about your mother?"

"Papa told me that she was beautiful and smart. He said

that she was very special." Her face turned sad. "But she was only seventeen and she couldn't take care of me." Silent tears streamed down her face. "He told me that he watched her through the little glass window the day I was born. He watched her crying in agony when the nurses took me away from her."

I watched her intently as I remembered the experience she was describing trying to hold back my own tears. "She wrapped me in a soft pink blanket, kissed the top of my head and she prayed over me. Papa said it was the single most beautiful thing he ever saw her do. Like it was some sort of sacred ritual."

I had prayed over her. My great-grandmother had taught me protection spells and I used the most powerful one I knew to send her out into her unknown future. I was glad that I had performed the protection ritual, especially since she ended up living with this family that seemed to have so many issues.

"All my life I've felt her love around me." She smiled as she wiped the tears from her face. "Did you know my mother?" Her expression turned hopeful.

"Yes." I nodded and began to regret guiding the conversation in this direction. I was not prepared to tell her that I was her mother without Marco's permission.

"Would you tell me about her?" she asked.

"I don't know, maybe I should make sure it's okay with your papa first."

"Please tell me something … anything," she pleaded hungry for information about the mother she never knew.

"Well, okay. Your mother did put a protection spell on you. She has the ability to heal the sick and a few other special talents. Her great-grandmother was a Brazilian Umbanda Priestess and she was training to follow in her footsteps."

"You mean like a witch?" Her eyes opened wide.

"No… not exactly, but I guess in a way some of what she can do is like witchcraft." I had never thought of myself as a witch, but more of a priestess like my great-grandmother. It always held a positive connotation for me.

"I wish she were here, maybe she could heal my grand-mother," she said.

I was so distracted by my own situation that I had not even thought of the possibility of healing Marco and Adriano's mother. She may have been too far gone with her cancer for me to heal her. I mostly healed infants and young women, but I certainly could give it a try.

"Let's get going so I can have a talk with your father about everything we've discussed."

Adriano and Marco were waiting for us when we returned home. It was obvious that they did not get along. They stood apart and barely looked at each other, unless it was with disdain. Elena kissed her father and uncle before running inside with her bags. I wondered if she was aware of the fact that they hated each other. I greeted both men. Adriano pulled me to him and kissed me passionately. I knew this kiss was not for my benefit. It had nothing to do with him and me. This kiss was purely to torture Marco. I gently pushed him away, trying not to upset him, but also trying to save

Marco from being constant witness to our intimacy.

"Did you have fun shopping?" Adriano asked as he looked up to see the jealously in his brother's eyes.

"Yes, we had a wonderful time. It was everything I imagined it would be." I looked at both men. "We need to talk." I motioned for them to follow me inside. I set my shopping bags on the marble chair side table in Marco's office. Adriano and Marco sat across from each other and I stood in between them.

"I want to tell her that I'm her mother." I chewed on my lower lip as I waited for their reactions.

"It's fine with me as long as you allow me to be there when you tell her." Marco said calmly.

"Gatinho, are you sure you want to do this? What if she gets upset?" Adriano asked.

"I talked to her today and she wants to know more about her mother. It was hard for me not to tell her earlier but I wanted Marco's permission," I explained.

"You have it." Marco smiled.

"I don't know why you are worried about him," Adriano complained. "He didn't ask your permission to adopt her and he certainly wasn't pining away for you when he bribed that man into dating you." *What?*

"He is her father. I couldn't take care of her. He had every right to raise her." I glared at Adriano almost wishing that looks could kill; then turned to Marco. "Thank you. She told me what you told her about me, but what is he talking about? Who did you bribe into dating me?" It had to be Rhett, but I just did not understand how that could be. Rhett's interest in me always seemed real. Then again, I did catch him with his face in Poppy's cleavage at our engagement party.

"Do we really have to talk about this now?" Marco asked.

"Yes, I have never needed help in the dating department. What is he talking about?" I asked pointing to his younger brother.

"I asked Rhett to keep an eye on you. I arranged for his tuition to be paid if he remained close to you," he admitted.

I had always wondered how Rhett had managed to get through medical school without needing loans. His family was not wealthy. We had been raised in similar middle-class homes. I had racked up quite a debt to finish medical school, but Rhett did not owe a dime the day we graduated.

"Why?" I asked calmly, but I was not really feeling calm. I was feeling controlled. Had he orchestrated the last 17 years of my life?

"I wanted to make sure you were taken care of. I liked him. He's a good man," he explained.

"So you thought you could control my love life?" I asked.

"I just wanted to keep you safe and happy." Marco explained. I should have been angry. I was angry, but Rhett had taken care of me, and now I understood that he had sacrificed his own happiness for years in order to take care of me for Marco. He had, of course, been well compensated, but in all of our years together we had been close friends and I knew in my heart that he would have taken care of me without the bribe. I nodded my understanding to Marco.

Adriano rose from his chair to stand possessively next to me with his hand around my waist ending Marco and I's moment of silent understanding. "There's something else we have to discuss. Well two things actually. First, I think you should allow her to date," I said.

"Biddy, I don't know…" Marco began to protest.

"You can't keep her locked up forever. She's not me, Marco," I interrupted. "I spoke to her about boys and the things that they want. She understands that she is too young for sex."

"I'll think about it." He rubbed the dark stubble on his chin. "What else did you want to discuss?"

"I want to try to heal your mother." Both men smiled. I got the feeling that they had discussed the possibility. It seemed to be one thing they could actually agree on.

"Could you do that, Gatinho?" Adriano asked hopefully.

"I don't know. I could try, but there is a problem."

"What?" Adriano asked.

"I'll need to take her into surgery. The diseased tissue needs to be removed and then I will perform the rituals. That's how I'm used to working. I don't want to take the chance of the cancer coming back."

"I'll talk to her. I'm sure I can convince her to let you do it. She knows how you healed my leg when I was a little boy," Adriano explained.

"Marco, would you get Elena, so we can talk to her while Adriano goes to speak to your mother?" I asked.

Marco nodded and left the room in search of our daughter. Adriano followed silently on his own mission.

My hands were shaking by the time Marco and Elena came back to his office. My daughter would finally know her mother. What was she going to do? Would she be angry? A hundred questions raced through my mind.

"Aunt Biddy, Papa says you both want to talk to me. Did you convince him to let me go on a date?" she asked unaware that dating was not the biggest issue to be dealt with at this moment.

"I don't know. Did I convince you, Marco?" I asked putting him on the spot. He frowned at me. I could tell that he didn't like being put on the spot in front of her about the dating issue.

"Yes, I will allow one date. You will go in the limo; that way I can send a bodyguard," he said giving in to us. Together my daughter and I had a powerful effect on his resolve.

Elena sighed.

"The body guard will sit in the front with the driver. You won't even know he's there," I offered. Elena immediately perked up to this solution and jumped into her father's arms for a hug.

"Thank you, Papa," Elena said and then sat on the edge of

the overstuffed leather arm chair nearest Marco.

"We have something more serious to discuss," Marco said trying to steer the conversation in the right direction. "Elena, I want you to know that I love you and nothing between us is going to change," he prefaced what we were about to reveal to her.

"Today, you asked me to tell you about your mother, but I didn't want to tell you too much without your father's permission," I began to say.

"Yes, I remember," she noted.

I paced back and forth working up the courage to spit out the words. I just need to say it out loud and it will be out in the open. I stopped pacing and moved close to her. "Elena, I am your mother." Elena gasped and stared open mouthed while she took in what I said. "I want you to know that when I put you up for adoption I felt I was doing the best I could do for you. It was the absolute hardest thing I've ever done. I loved you then and I still love you now."

Marco moved to wrap his arms around her for support. "Are you okay?" he asked his daughter.

"I knew it." She smiled. "I knew it the moment I looked at you." She busted free from her father's hold and rushed towards me with open arms almost knocking me over with the force of her embrace. I held my daughter in my arms for the first time since the day she was born. All those years my arms had ached for her. Tears streamed down my face as Marco stepped towards us, wiping my tears and embracing us both in is strong arms. I'll never forget this moment. The sheer joy of holding my long lost daughter

and finding my one true love again was overwhelming. We were together. Our situation was not perfect, but it was still better than being apart.

"You will be mine again. We will be a family," he whispered in my ear.

"Papa, you're squeezing too hard." Elena gasped for air between us. He released us. We all stared at each other not knowing what to do next.

"Can I call you Mae or Mom?" Elena asked eagerly.

"Yes, whichever you like." The word coming from her mouth was like angels singing.

"Well, isn't this a heart-warming picture perfect moment," Adriano sneered sarcastically, as he leaned against the door frame.

"Adriano, behave," I scolded his immaturity.

"Are you ready for bed, Gatinho?" His arms were folded across his chest.

"I'll be up in a minute," I replied sharply.

"I'll wait for you." He stood waiting for me. He was downright obstinate.

"Mom, does this mean you can use your healing powers to cure Grandmother?" Elena asked.

"Yes, she agreed to the surgery," Adriano replied.

"One of you will have to speak to the hospital about my

use of their operating room. I will need the usual staff of nurses, an anesthesiologist, and a general surgeon."

"I'll take care of it," Marco replied. "I'm on the hospital board of directors."

"Great. I have to say good night now, but I'll see you tomorrow and we can talk about what you'll wear on your date." I hugged my daughter one more time. Elena's smile beamed and hugged me back.

"Good night, Mom." Elena watched as I stepped toward my husband. Marco wrapped his arms around Elena as she wished me good night. They both looked happy, but Marco's face also clearly displayed the jealousy and sadness that he was trying to hide.

Adriano reached out for my hand and pulled me to him, sliding his hand over my backside suggestively, another gesture for his brother's benefit. I had no plans of having sex with him—ever. I still felt his magnetic pull, but I wanted to save my love and body for Marco.

The Offer

I woke to find Adriano's side of the bed empty and cold. He had fazed and ran out on me last night after I told him that I still did not want to make love.

"Momma, Momma. Wake-up." Elena called out as she knocked heavily on my door. "I'm going on my first date tonight. We have to get ready."

"I'm coming." I jumped out of the bed and swung the door open to her smiling overexcited face. "First of all, go eat breakfast, and then we'll worry about getting ready." I was giving mommy orders already. It was a great feeling.

"Okay, Momma." She turned to go then turned back around. "I love the sound of that, Momma."

"Me, too. Say it again," I requested, with what I imagined was the silliest grin ever.

"Momma," she repeated and returned a silly smile.

"Breakfast now. If you don't mind, please bring me something to eat when you're done and then we'll look through your closet and have a more thorough talk about boys." She nodded again and ran down the stairs to breakfast. I shut the door and turned back into the room slamming face first into my naked husband in a state of full arousal.

"Good morning, Gatinho." He ran the back of is warm hand down my cheek and then wrapped his hand around my neck. "You look rested. Did you sleep well?" he asked softly as he lowered his lips to lightly brush the tender skin behind my ear. He knew how to push all my buttons. His touch created a gentle shiver that went down my spine.

"Yes, very well." I had slept like a baby. No dreams, no interruptions.

"Didn't you miss me? I hoped you would've had some trouble sleeping without me." I had not missed him because I was too focused on trying to think of ways to be with Marco.

"I guess my mind was just preoccupied with thoughts of Elena." I put my hands on his chest to push him away, but he didn't budge an inch.

"And Marco," he added as he slid his leg between my thighs. I did not respond to his obvious attempt at upsetting me, but I could feel his jealousy. He lowered his hand to my thigh and ran his palm slowly and deliberately up the outside of my leg until his hand was cupping the bottom curve of my backside.

"Mmm…" he moaned. "You have such a nice ass," he growled, appreciatively. His was starting to become even more aggressive in his attempts to shake me from my denial of him in the bedroom.

"Elena will be back any minute. We have mother daughter time planned for the whole day," I informed him, steeling my resolve not to give into him and his deliciously perfect body.

"You know I'm starting to feel neglected, my love. I had plans for us that you cancelled and you promised to make it up to me—but you haven't." He pushed the straps of my night gown off my shoulders and smiled as the silky fabric slid down my body falling onto the floor. He kissed his mark on my bare shoulder reaching behind me to lock the door. "My ego needs stroking, Gatinho." By the looks of it, there were other things that needed stroking and I wasn't sure how to avoid his sexual advances this time. He lifted me into his arms and carried me to our bed. He gently laid me among the soft blankets before lying next to me. His copper eyes surveyed my body as if I was a banquet feast and he was trying to decide where to start.

He lowered his mouth lightly brushing his lips across mine. "I want to make you pregnant. I can give you a baby. You'll never have to give it away. We can raise it together." His warm hand stroked circles across my abdomen.

I wanted another child, but I did not want it with him. I took my birth control faithfully, so I knew there was not much of a chance of us getting pregnant at this time. And I knew he really wanted the child so he could gain control of his family's empire and rid himself of his brother once and for all. I gasped as his fingers began a slow torturous decent. I resisted the reactions of my body to his kiss and hands, but my body gave away at the obvious pleasure he created with his touch. Moans periodically escaped my lips.

"You will finally be mine," he moaned has he shifted his body over mine. Just as he was sure of my inability to no longer refuse him, someone knocked on the door. He groaned in frustration muttering in Portuguese something that sounded like an expletive.

"Go away. We're in the middle of something," he yelled at the person behind the door. I frowned at the tone of voice he was using with Elena. "Come back this afternoon."

"Do you really think it'll take that long?" I mumbled under my breath.

"If you're a good girl." He lifted his body slightly and was about to thrust himself fully inside me when I quickly rolled out from under him off of the bed and onto the floor. Pain shot up my leg, causing me to scream at the intensity of sensation.

"What's the matter with you?" he asked.

I think we were both shocked that I had actually flung myself on the floor. My leg was hurting. He lowered himself beside me and pulled my limp body close to him. I could feel what he was feeling. It was a mixture of confusion, rejection and love. The last emotion made it difficult for me to totally freak out on him. Feeling his love for me from the inside out was overpowering. It did not allow me to feel much else. This tool of his was definitely the strongest weapon he would have to keep me under his power.

"Why won't you make love to me?" he asked.

"Because I love Marco," I replied, honestly.

"Well, if you give me the child I want, I'll let him have you," he said, running his fingers through his hair in exasperation.

I just stared at him, so it really wasn't me at all that he wanted, but this was confusing because I could feel that he loved me. Maybe I was confusing love with lust. I guess his feelings for me, whatever they might be, were not as powerful as his desire to please his father or out do his brother.

"I need to heal my leg. Can you go run me a bath?" I asked.

"Will you think about it?" he asked. "Give me the baby I want, and I'll release you."

"What if the child is like Elena? What if it doesn't have either of our abilities?" I asked.

"Then we will have to keep trying until we get it right," he said.

I just shook my head. His request was a genetic lottery that would not likely come out in my favor.

"Bath please?" I asked.

"Just think about it," he said before rising to run my bathwater.

I reached down and massaged my twisted ankle and proceeded to evoke the prayers of healing.

My cell phone buzzed signaling the arrival of an email. I slowly crawled from the floor up to the bedside table, grabbing my phone on the way to the shower. Once alone, I scrolled through the apps on my phone and opened the mail icon. The email was from

Dixie with the subject line of '*You are not really married.*'

I opened the email: *You're marriage is not legal. See the attached news story. Come home. I miss you. Love, Dixie.* I opened the attachment to find an article with a picture of Cookie and her husband. I read through the story. Dixie was right. I was not married to Adriano, by U.S. law anyway. Cookie's husband had lost his license allowing him to perform marriages. All of the marriages he had performed over the past year were not legal. As far as Adriano was concerned, he also believed we were married by the law of his people. That is what the scar on my shoulder was far, but at least legally I was free. I hoped it would make it easier for Marco to help me.

I composed an email back to Dixie.

Thanks for the article. Things are more complicated than that. Marco is here, and I've found my daughter. I'll keep you posted. Love, Biddy.

She was the only person, besides my parents, who knew about Marco and my daughter. I trusted her to keep those secrets so many years ago and she had remained loyal to her word.

Noni's Help

After deleting Dixie's email, I bathed in the large garden tub and concentrated on what to do next. I lit several jasmine scented candles and placed them around the tub. The hot water surrounding my body felt good. I wanted it to wash away my sins. To take away all the wrong I had done to Elena and all the men in my life. I felt responsible for all of their anguish; even though I logically knew that they had a hand in their own fates as well. I listened for Adriano's movements in the bedroom. He was not moving around so he must have left the room. Even though it scared me to death, I reached out with my mind to his and tested this link between us. To my surprise the main feeling in his mind was hope. I figured this hope hinged on him feeling like I would take him up on his offer to have a child with him. It made sense because from his viewpoint I did not have much of a choice.

What he did not know was that I would never be willing to give up a child again. I learned my lesson in giving up Elena all those years ago. I would not be making that same mistake again. I put his offer out of my mind because it was something I would not be considering.

I closed my eyes and concentrated on nothingness. Noni

had taught me how to bring myself to this place in order to seek out prophesy. It is not something I practiced often. My life in Kentson had been relatively normal. There was never really a need for contacting the dead. I felt my body fall asleep first. Then my mind entered that place between awake and sleep. This place was powerful because it allowed for interaction of the living and the dead.

"Noni," I called out into my mind. "I need help. Please send me a vision or a sign to answer my questions." I did not have to wait long. The first image I saw was the bar where I had first met Adriano. The image of him fixing drinks for me at the bar. Then the vision fast forwarded to his handing me wine at the restaurant in Las Vegas. Each vision was run in alternating segments of fast and slow motion that allowed me to see him putting a small amount of liquid from a vial in each drink. Once my mind was clear on what the visions meant, that he had been using a love potion of some kind, the vision switched to images of Noni's village. Pictures of me walking down the gravel paths between houses and finding the priestess called Zamora. The priestess was waiting for me. Her skin was tanned by the sun. Her hair was long and black. It waved in the breeze as she motioned to me to come forward.

"Gatinho, wake-up." Adriano shook my shoulder gently as he spoke. "Elena wants to talk to you." When I opened my eyes, the candles were no longer burning.

"Please tell her I'll meet her in her room." I stood from my bath water and reached for a large fluffy white towel. Adriano handed me the muffin that Elena had brought for my breakfast. It was odd to me that I was not embarrassed to be naked in front of Adriano. The only thing that made sense was that it must be another side effect of his love bites. A jaguar male would want his female to feel ultimately comfortable and safe with him.

"I already did. She also brought you some coffee. It's on your night table." He grabbed my towel and wrapped me up in its soft warmth.

"So are you feeling better now?" he asked, as he turned on the shower.

"Much better." I was definitely better now that I was starting to use my powers to figure out what he was up to.

"Can I ask you a question?" I asked, before taking a bite out of my muffin. He nodded in agreement. "Can you feel what I'm feeling?" He stepped closer brushing his lips slowly across my cheek.

"Do you like that little effect of my bites, Gatinho?"

"It's interesting, but can you feel it, too?" I bit down onto my muffin again, hoping that he could not feel my emotions.

"Yes, I can feel what you are feeling. I can't read your thoughts, but I feel it when you are happy, sad, or any other emotion. It also allows us to tell when the other is lying. It's especially strong when you're in my arms, but…" he paused in thought. "Like last night, I felt your excitement when Elena accepted you so quickly and when Marco held you in his arms." That definitely explained his bad mood the night before.

"I only started to feel it recently. Why is that?"

"Probably because of your limited jaguar genes or maybe

because I drink your blood each time. It's more potent. You only receive small doses of my saliva. You see, Gatinho, it is like we are one." He wrapped his strong arms around me and kissed my shoulder and collarbone.

"I know you were drugging me." I felt his surprise and his body tense. "What is it that you have been putting in my drinks?"

"How do you know this?" he loosened his hold to look into my eyes. Then it occurred to me that he did not know the full range of my talents. He probably thought that I was just a healer.

"I had a vision." He was nervous now. I had caught him in a position that he would rather not be in. "Don't forget, you can't lie to me. I'll know if you are." This emotional link had its benefits.

"I was just speeding up the process. You would've been mine regardless." He stroked his fingers through my long hair. "And I haven't given it to you since we've been married."

"What was it?" I asked through gritted teeth.

"A love potion. I got it from a woman in your ancestors' village when I was checking into your background." He looked smug, but apparently he did not get all of my background information. "I knew I only needed it until I could mark you. I'm supposed to be able to just touch you and have you melt for me; our link as mates is much stronger than that witch's love potion. What I didn't expect was that your powers allow you to control your feelings for me." To prove his point he unwrapped my towel and ran his fingers from my lower lip down my neck and all the way to my…oh my.

"Hmm…" I moaned. The feeling intensified because I could now feel his desire as well as my own. The corner of his mouth rose ever so slightly at my reaction to his touch.

"Adriano, you do realize that this artificial attraction that you've created between us is not as powerful as true love." I said, as he wrapped me back up in my towel. He knotted the side of the towel around me tightly. My words angered him. I could feel the slow seething anger and hurt that melded at the core of him.

"If you want to be with Marco, he and I will have to fight to the death. One of us will die. Can you live with that?" He stared into my eyes not allowing me to look away.

"Can you live with the fact that I don't love you? I love him." I pulled away from him. "All this mind control and love potion business might have worked on an average woman or even a jaguar woman, but I have my own powers. My mind is especially strong." I turned toward the door standing in the doorframe to finish my thought. "You might be able to have my body melt for you, but you'll never have my heart."

I stormed out throwing the rest of my muffin away. I no longer had an appetite. I dressed in jean shorts and a white T-shirt. I could feel his anger growing inside of us and it fueled my determination to be free of his control.

Elena was waiting for me in her bedroom. Marco was also sitting in the corner reading the newspaper. He lowered the paper when I entered the room. Elena's bed was covered in clothing. It looked like a tornado had hit her room.

"Good morning. Did you both sleep well?" I stepped closer

and Elena hugged me. Marco nodded and went back to reading his paper.

"Mom, my date is taking me to dinner and to the school dance. What should I wear?" she asked as I looked over the pile of clothes.

"Maybe we should clean up first. We might find the perfect thing in the process." I lifted a shirt off the pile and searched for a hanger. Elena immediately started to do the same.

"Marco, did you speak to the hospital?" I asked as we cleaned up Elena's mess.

"Yes, tomorrow there is an opening. I came by to tell you earlier but your husband said that you were busy." He looked angry. I groaned inwardly. Marco heard me scream. He probably assumed it was from sex. I would have to find a way to let him know that I had not still succumbed to Adriano's attempts to consummate our marriage.

"I'm sorry that I couldn't see you earlier. It was beyond my control." I looked at him hoping to lighten his mood. He shook his head, but continued to frown.

"We will bring her in first thing in the morning. You can start the surgery at seven. Is this the kind of medicine you usually practice?" he asked. *Was he doubting me?*

"Yes, I am used to performing surgery if that is what you're getting at. I do c-sections and tubal ligations, regularly. I trained first to be a surgeon, but I felt death to often in the operating room. I wanted to be the kind of doctor that could use my extra healing ability regularly." They both looked at me perplexed. "If Death is ready to take the patient, it is not recommended for me to use my abilities to prevent him from taking the soul."

"You have that kind of power?" Marco looked at me disbelieving. "You have the power to stop Death from taking a soul."

"Well, I've never done it, but yes." I looked at them both and sat on the now nearly cleaned bed. "If I were to do such a thing, it would have unnatural consequences."

They both stared at me in silence. I continued picking up clothes. This child has way too much clothing. At the bottom of the pile was a pretty black dress. It was simple. Short sleeves that puffed at the shoulder and the dress tapered at the waist. The skirt flared at little above the knee. I lifted the dress and smiled.

"This is it." I turned Elena towards the mirror and held it up in front of her. "We'll put your hair up and put on just a little make-up." I smiled at her reflection in the mirror. She smiled back.

"Oh, Momma, it's perfect." She took the dress and laid it flat on her now clean bed.

"Okay, we have plenty of time until you need to get ready. So find something to do to take your mind off of your date until then." I turned to Marco. "We need to talk privately, where no one can hear us." I pointed towards Adriano's room. He nodded in understanding, grabbed me by the elbow, and turned towards Elena's door. We quickly walked outside to his car.

Marco parked the car in a secluded area that we had visited many years ago. It was at least a thirty minute drive from his home.

He shut off the engine and turned to me. He was so handsome. I wanted to reach out and rub my fingers across the red birthmark on his face, but I had to control my emotions to avoid alerting Adriano to anything odd.

"What do you want to talk about?" Marco asked his voice still apprehensive.

"I received an email from a friend back home. I'm not legally married to your brother. The man who performed the ceremony was not licensed to do so."

"Does Adriano know about this?" A smile settled on his lips.

"No." I lifted my fingers and ran them across his mouth. "I also found out that he drugged me with a love potion from my own people. That is how he was able to make me think I wanted him so badly."

"So you don't want him anymore?" he asked. He was unsure of my feelings. I just wanted to shake him. I wanted to scream at him. *Can't you see that you are the man that I love? That there has never been anyone else that has held me captive the way that you do.* However, I was trying not to get overly excited. I did not want Adriano phasing into a jaguar and tracking me down.

"Oh, my body still wants him. That saliva thing that you people do is strong, but I told him this morning that I didn't love him. That he could have my body but not my heart." Marco moved closer, holding my head in his warm hand. The feeling of his fingers on my neck had me shivering. "My heart is yours, if you want it."

"I want it, but I also want the rest of you. It turned my stomach when I heard you scream in his arms this morning. I want to be the one who brings you that kind of pleasure."

"I'm so sorry," I squeaked, as I began to cry. "I screamed from twisting my ankle when I rolled out from under him just before he was about to … you know …"

"So you still haven't made love to him?" he asked, relief clear in his tone.

"No, it's been difficult but I've managed not to succumb to him. It's especially hard when I feel how badly he desires it." I looked into his worried eyes. "He truly believes that he loves me. Do you know how hard it is to refuse someone when you can feel how much they want you?"

"No, I don't know what that's like. I'm sorry. I know this is hard for you, too." I was relieved to know that he had never shared this link with anyone. That meant that he had never marked a female. This information made me happy.

"I want to be with you and only you. I want it to be your body next to mine at night, holding me. I want it to be you waking me up to make love to you." I lifted his hand and placed it over my heart. "When you used to make love to me, it was love. I felt it in every cell of my body. I didn't need magic to feel it. I want to feel that way again." His lips touched mine and fire burned between us. He pulled me into his lap. Our bodies clung together as we kissed. The need in me ached for release. Then I felt it, I felt a roar of anger. Adriano was aware of my intense feeling of carnal need and he knew it was not for him.

"We have to stop." I sighed breathlessly. "He knows what we're doing. I can feel his anger." Marco's lips fell from mine and I moved back into the passenger seat. I focused on calming my need for Marco. As my breathing returned to normal, I turned to look at him. He was watching me. His desire to finish what we started burned through me.

"Take me to the village. There is someone I need to see," I instructed. I needed to find the priestess. Zamora would know what to do.

We parked on the outskirts of the village and walked through the gravel and dirt paths just like I had seen in my vision. One small wooden house stood out to me. I knocked on the door and a woman opened it. It was the priestess in my vision.

"I've been waiting for you, Biddy. Come in." She waved us into her home.

"Zamora, I need your help."

"Noni told me your problems. She visited me this morning." She motioned for us to take a seat at the small table in her kitchen.

"Me, too. She told me to find you."

Marco just looked between the two of us, without saying a word.

Zamora glanced at Marco. "This is not the one you wish to be rid of. He is much too handsome. You must keep him."

"This is Marco; I would like very much to keep him. That is why I need your help. Another man has me under his control." She

stood next to me and pulled down the corner of my t-shirt to reveal the large scare on my shoulder. "You've allowed the jaguar to mark you; that is serious." She turned to Marco.

"If you love this woman, you know what you must do to free her from this other man's control."

Marco nodded.

"But they are brothers. I don't want him to kill his own brother," I pleaded. I didn't want him to kill anyone for me. "Is there no other way?"

"There is another way. If the one who marked you were to betray you. If he mates with another, then you can break from him. You are supposed to mate for life, but if either of you strays, the bond is in question, leaving the betrayed mate to decide the fate of the relationship. The males usually choose to kill the other male involved. It is an accepted end to the conflict among the jaguar people. But all this is rare; jaguar women don't tend to have feelings for any other men. Their mate usually sees to that. Does he not bite you each time you mate?"

"He bites me, but we have never mated. He tricked me and marked me without my consent. I love Marco. I always have and I always will."

Zamora gasped. "I've never heard of a woman who could overcome the intense power of the jaguar's mark. You must be extremely powerful," she remarked, with reverence. "Well, it sounds like you know what you have to do. Either you trick him into betraying you or Marco ends his life."

"Is there anything you can do to help me trick him?" I asked.

She walked over to a wooden shelf and grabbed a bottle of something and handed it to me. I was wishing that I would have paid more attention to Noni's lessons.

"This potion is very powerful. With it and a little of your blood, you can make another woman look like you and sound like you. It will not last long, so the woman will have to work quickly to make sure she seduces him fully." She finished by teaching me the spell to make the potion work.

"Do you know of a woman who would be willing to help us?" I asked. She shook her head. She did not know of anyone who would be willing to risk the extreme danger of angering a shape shifter.

"I know the perfect woman for the job," Marco spoke up. "There is an old girlfriend of his that wouldn't mind taking a little revenge."

"Okay, well then, it's settled. You'll drop me off at home to help Elena get ready for her date and then you can find this woman. Arrange for her to be your date for tonight. The four of us will have dinner and at some point we'll conduct the switch. Make sure she understands that she has to have sex with him. Pay her if you have to. Do whatever it takes." We thanked Zamora for her help. I made no offer of money, because it would have been an insult to pay for this type of service. I would send her an offering of fruit and spices.

Once back at the plantation, I went straight to Elena's

room. She was waiting rather impatiently. She had already bathed and was sitting at her vanity unrolling the large hot rollers from her hair. I walked up behind her and finished taking the now cool rollers from her hair. Each large smooth curl bounced as it was released.

"I see you didn't need your mother to figure out how to get this wild hair of ours under control." I said as I ran my fingers through the thick mane of soft brown curls.

"No, Aunt Adriana bought these for me when I was twelve. She taught me how to use them." She went on telling me how each of her aunts and her grandmother had been there when she needed help. She told me a story about how horrified she was the day she started her period. All the other girls at school had their mothers to talk to and that was one of the days that she really wished I had been around. All the older women in the house had gone on a vacation. She had to ask her father for help. He drove her to the store and gave her his credit card while he sat out in the parking lot waiting for her get what she needed. The problem was she really did not know what she needed. His eyes just about fell out of his head when she walked out of the store with a bag full of different brands and kinds of feminine supplies. He paid one of the maids to go through the bag with her and explain it all. We spent some time giggling about his reaction.

I pulled her hair up into a ponytail and then went on fixing it into a pretty up do with curls pinned around the top of her head. She put on her dress and then sat back down for me to apply her makeup. Then she began asking questions about my relationship with her father.

I told her about how we met. I remembered that day fondly. I was shopping in the market looking at a beautiful necklace that one of the local vendors had on display. I stood staring at it, but I did not have enough money to buy the necklace and the food that I was supposed to be gathering for my great-grandmother. So I moved on and went about the business of picking the fruits and vegetables she had sent me out to purchase. When I passed back to look at the necklace one last time, I noticed it was gone. Some lucky tourists must have bought it, I thought. When I stepped to the edge of the market towards the village, there was the most handsome boy staring at me with those mysterious copper eyes. He spoke to me, but I did not understand what he was saying. My family had never taught me to speak Portuguese. When I just stared back at him, he spoke again in English. He introduced himself to me and asked if he could give me a gift. My family had taught me not to take gifts from strangers, so I politely refused. Then he asked if he could escort me home. I really thought he was the dreamiest boy I had ever met, so I allowed him to take the packages I was holding and walk with me. We talked all the way back to the village. When we were just on the outer edge of the houses, he stopped and asked if I would meet him that night at the festival near the marketplace. I agreed and took the packages back from him and continued on to Noni's house. Every few steps I would turn around to see if he was still standing there. Each time, I was not disappointed. He stood there and watched me until I was on the small wooden porch of Noni's little house.

I told Noni about Marco. There were no secrets between the old woman and me. I asked her if I could go to the festival and she agreed as long as he would escort me back home. I did not think he

would mind. That night when I got to the edge of the village I saw him walking towards me.

"I hope you don't mind but I wanted to make sure you would be safe walking to the festival," he said shyly.

"I don't mind." I smiled as he extended his hand to take mine. Electricity flowed between us as we held hands.

We enjoyed the festival. We ate and walked around looking at the art on display. I insisted we pass near the jewelry maker to see if there was another necklace. I had brought enough money with me, just in case she had made another one. There was none. When the music started, he asked me to dance. We danced and danced until my feet hurt. When the festival was over, we began the walk back to the village. We were about half way there, when he stopped walking and pulled a small white box with a slender blue bow out of his pocket. He put it into my hands and insisted that since we were no longer strangers that I could accept his gift. I pulled the bow off the box and lifted the lid to find the necklace that I had wanted so badly. I must have been smiling from ear to ear because he looked so pleased with my reaction. He lifted the necklace from the box and placed it around my neck. It was a silver chain with a solid black stone set into a sliver pendant.

He took my hand and we finished our walk to the village. This time he walked me all the way to Noni's porch stopping in front of the steps.

"Thank you, Marco. You have no idea how disappointed I was when I saw it had been purchased." I touched the necklace. "I love it."

"I tried to put you out of your misery earlier, but you wouldn't accept it," he replied as he touched the stone and allowed his hand to touch my neck. My skin tingled as his fingers trailed up my neck and cupped my face. He brought his other hand to rest on the opposite side of my face and he stared down into my eyes. His eyes closed as he slowly moved his mouth closer to mine. The moment his lips touched mine I knew that I was in love. His kiss was gentle and sweet. He made no effort to part my lips or extend the kiss any further. He slowly lifted his mouth from mine and opened his eyes. I stood there in awe. He simply told me good-night and promised to find me the next day.

By the time I finished the story, Elena's make-up was finished and she was ready to go on her first date. She put on some simple silver earrings and a bracelet that matched. She was beautiful. I reminded her about boys and about not letting her hormones control her. She agreed.

"Momma, whatever happened to that necklace?" she asked.

"She threw it at me when I broke her heart," Marco explained as he entered her room. "She hit me right in the face with it. It hurt for days. I even had a bruise." I bit down on my lip to keep from laughing.

"Go, Momma," Elena said. "Serves you right, Papa. If you wouldn't have broken her heart you wouldn't be so miserable and lonely." He pulled the necklace from his pocket and placed it around Elena's neck. He put his mouth close to her ear. "I'm working on fixing everything." She smiled, I smiled, and he smiled. It was contagious. "You're so beautiful … just like your mother." He kissed her lightly on the cheek. "Your date's here. He's waiting downstairs."

"You didn't say anything embarrassing to him did you, Papa?" Elena nervously fingered the necklace that now hung around her neck.

"I just showed him my gun collection." He shrugged. "Was that too much?" Marco chuckled mostly to himself. She ran out the room toward the stairs with a look of complete horror on her pretty face.

"Please tell me you are joking about the guns," I asked.

"Yes." He rolled his eyes and we followed Elena down the stairs. I watched him stroll confidently behind our daughter.

At the bottom of the stairs was a tall, handsome teenage boy. He had short spiky red hair and eyes as blue as the ocean. He stared open mouthed at Elena as she walked down the stairs. They awkwardly greeted each other and he slipped a pretty white flowered corsage onto her wrist. I giggled at the old fashioned custom. Apparently kids still did that sort of thing for school dances. Elena turned to introduce us to her date.

"Momma and Papa, this is Ferdinand, but everyone calls him Fern." She lifted the white flowers on her wrist for me to inspect more closely.

"Hello, Fern. It's nice to meet you." I smiled at the handsome boy hoping to ease his nerves. "Please have Elena home right after the dance."

"Oh, I know. Mr. Barnardos already gave me instructions." He smiled nervously. "Thanks again for letting us use the limo."

They turned to go and Marco nodded to the two men waiting outside with the limo. I recognized the driver but the larger more menacing figure was a man that I had never seen before. He was tall and overly muscled. I imagined his name would be Killer or No Neck Nick.

"Please don't tell me you've got an armed guard in the limo?" I motioned to the car outside as Elena and Fern slid into the backseat of the car.

"I have to protect my baby." He folded his strong arms in front of his chest.

"That poor kid is too nervous to hurt her and besides your judging him based on how smooth you were at his age. She'll be lucky if he works up the courage to shake her hand much less kiss her."

"That's exactly what I was hoping for," he quipped as one corner of his mouth worked itself into a devilish smirk.

"Sheesh." I rolled my eyes. "You growled at him, didn't you? You didn't show him any guns, but I have the strong feeling that you growled your scary jaguar growl at him." He didn't say a word, but his little smirk turned into a full toothy grin. "Marco, you are not allowed to growl at any of her dates unless they have threatened her." We watched as the limo left the front driveway. "Is your date coming over for dinner tonight?"

"Yes, dinner is in an hour."

The Switch

Adriano was waiting for me when I returned to our room to dress for dinner. He did not speak at first. He just watched me as he buttoned his shirt. I knew he was angry and curious. I had been feeling it all day. I knew he would ask me at some point why I had experienced such extreme sensations of desire while I was not with him. I was not going to bring it up. I undressed and selected a simple blue dress for the evening. I picked through the drawer where I had placed my underwear until I found a matching bra and panty set that would leave no panty line under the clingy material of my dress. Adriano stood behind me and unsnapped my bra. I pulled it off and put on the new one. He flipped me around to face him.

"Did you make love to him today?" he asked straight forward and simple. His eyes searching mine for an answer that would allow him the revenge that he desired.

"You are my husband and until that status changes, I will not sleep with him." What I really wanted to say was that I really wanted to be with Marco and it was tempting to just let them fight it out to the death.

The goal of the evening was for my look alike to seduce him, so I figured it was best to get him on my good side. He sat in one of the chairs in the corner of the room and watched me put on my dress and brush my hair. He believed me because he knew I was speaking the truth. His mood became smoldering and desirous as we watched each other through the mirror of the vanity where I sat brushing my hair. I knew that if I could hold him off until after dinner, that there was a good chance that the other woman would be able to pull off her seduction.

"I'm ready for diner," I said as I walked to the chair where he was sitting. He pulled me down into his lap and kissed me. His emotion overwhelmed me. It was like drowning in desire. If I let him he would totally consume me. I finally broke free long enough to insist that we join everyone else at dinner. I had to promise that we would be alone to discuss his offer as soon as dinner ended.

In the dining room everyone was waiting for us including a beautiful Brazilian bombshell. She was perfectly tanned and impeccably dressed. She reminded me of a bronze version of Poppy. I felt the mix of emotion surge through Adriano as he gazed at her. He was surprised, which I expected, but there was also suspicion and something that felt an awful lot like love. I was not sure who the feelings of love were directed towards. He always had this particular sentiment at the surface of his emotions so it was not new to the mix but seemed stronger than usual. Marco had mentioned that the two lovers had parted unamiacably. A little mind reading would come in handy right now, but unfortunately, that was not part of our relationship.

"Biddy, I'd like you to meet my date for this evening. This is Luciana." I held back a chuckle. Luciana was the perfect name for this beautiful creature. Her name spoken with his accent felt like

velvet in my ears. I always wanted a name that could arouse a man on its own. Biddy was the name of an old lady in a bingo hall not a powerful physic priestess.

"Hello, it's nice to meet you, Luciana," I said as I bowed my head slightly in greeting. She smiled and mimicked my gesture.

"Hello, Biddy … Adriano. It's been a long time. Marco has told me of your recent marriage. Congratulations to you both." Luciana spoke gracefully.

"Thank you. We are very happy." He gazed at me, fully aware that I was feeling every emotion that he felt. Right now there was a tinge of desire and regret. So he definitely still had feelings for this woman. *Interesting.*

Dinner progressed as usual. We ate and talked. Every-one seemed to have a generally wonderful time. The particularly painful part was feeling the spike of jealously Adriano would feel every time Marco would put his hand on Luciana. Marco was deliberately baiting his brother. An eye for an eye. Throughout the evening he had bent down and kissed her cheek, neck, and even the skin behind her ear. He put on a good show. He spent time holding her hand and caressing her arm with his fingers. He almost had me convinced that they were an item, but I knew better. I knew in my heart that he was mine. If he would have wanted this woman or any other for that matter, he would be married to her by now. He had had many years to find a permanent replacement for me.

After dinner, I told Adriano to meet me in the bed room with some wine to finish what we had started earlier. I kissed him slowly, licking his lips to intensify the animalistic longing I was trying to project through my emotions. He nodded, biting my lower lip.

Marco had already taken Luciana upstairs to my room to get ready to drink the potion. She was naked on the bed when I walked in. *Wow.* I surveyed her perfect body. No tan lines, no cellulite, and perfect perky full breasts. *He gave her up for me? Wow.* So I handed her the potion that I mixed with my blood earlier and she drank it. I chanted the ritual over her and watched in amazement as I looked down on myself. I slid out of the room and into Marco's room across the hall.

We stood in silence. I tried not to even breathe because I knew that Adriano would be able to hear the slightest noise I made. We listened as the door to my room opened. Adriano was inside with Luciana. We went into the bathroom and turned on the shower so we could talk; hoping that the white noise of the shower would disguise our voices.

"What's going on?" he asked me.

"I don't know." I shrugged. "I can't read his mind. I can just feel his emotions. Right now he is feeling very horny." I rolled my eyes. "The man lives in a constant state of horny."

"Most men do, Biddy," he said, then grabbed me and kissed me. We lingered in each other's arms taking turns kissing each other's faces. I kissed his birthmark sweetly just like I used to do when we first started seeing each other. Then he grabbed my head and kissed me urgently … hungry for more.

"We have to stop," I gasped as his hands grazed up the outside of my thighs.

"Why? He's doing the same thing," he justified.

"I promised him I wouldn't sleep with you until I was free of him," I explained. He released me and we sat on the floor facing each other. A few short minutes passed and then I felt an intense release of anger. Whoa! I was supposed to feel a totally different kind of release from Adriano's mind. This could not be good. Instinctively, I knew exactly what this meant.

"Crap." I looked at Marco. "He figured it out."

He turned off the shower and we walked out into his bedroom. Maybe I could still make this work, if I got to the bedroom fast enough I could accuse him of cheating. It would be hard to deny if they are both still naked. I ran to my bedroom door and flung it open.

"Just what do you think you're doing with my husband?" I yelled at Luciana who still looked exactly like me. Adriano was sitting on the edge of the bed still fully dressed. Luciana was sitting next to him crying, babbling in Portuguese.

"Gatinho, would you mind explaining this to me?" He pointed to Luciana. "You may have been able to change her appearance, but there are other things about her that you couldn't change."

"Like what?" I asked out of morbid curiosity.

"Like the fact that when I kissed her I didn't feel her emotions change." He stood and walked to me touching my face while he spoke. "When I kiss you and touch you, your emotions fill me. We had it going for a few minutes then it just stopped." He looked suspiciously at me. "When I asked you...er...her...why she wasn't feeling anything, she just started crying and yelling at me in Portuguese about breaking her heart. I definitely knew it wasn't you after all that."

I should have thought of that. Of course, he would not have felt what she was feeling. If I had only not stopped Marco from making love to me, then we would have pulled this plan off.

Marco came into the room behind me. He spoke sharply at Luciana in Portuguese. I really needed to learn the language. It sounded pretty rough. She dressed and made her way to the door.

"I'm the one who visited the priestess for the potion to change Luciana. I wanted to trick you so that your union with Biddy wouldn't be valid and I could take her away from you." Marco pulled Luciana into the hallway. "By the way, she's not your legal wife. I've done some digging and the marriage license isn't valid." He slammed the door shut.

"What is he talking about?" Adriano stepped closer to embrace me. He wrapped his arms around my waist and peered into my eyes.

"The man who performed our marriage wasn't properly licensed." I went on to explain the email I had received from Dixie.

"Why didn't you tell me?" He looked and felt angry. Extremely angry.

"Does it really matter?" I touched the mark on my shoulder. "Our other bond is legal to your people."

"Our people," he corrected. "You may not be able to shift,

but you have jaguar blood, too. I can taste it." Then he leaned down and bit my neck. It was a small bite and he made quick work of healing it.

"Listen, I'm tired and I have to perform your mother's surgery in the morning. Would you mind if I slept in Elena's room? I'd like to be there when she comes home from her date."

"I'd really prefer if you slept here with me." He stroked the side of my face and kissed the top of my head.

"I'm sorry. I just can't. Wake me up at five am. I need time to focus before the surgery," I instructed.

Elena came in a little after midnight. She turned on the light and quickly shut it off when she realized I was sleeping in her bed. I turned on the lamp on her nightstand, so she could see what she was doing. She slid into her pajamas and in the bed next to me. By the expression on her face, I could tell that her date had gone well.

"So how was your first date? Was Fern a gentleman?"

"Yes, a perfect gentleman. I think he's scared of Papa." I would be too if Papa Jaguar growled at me.

"Tell me everything." She went on to tell me literally every detail. "Let's get to the important part. Did he kiss you goodnight?"

"Yes, he walked me to the door, and when he said good-night, he kissed me!" She giggled. "Oh, it was the most romantic experience of my life." I stifled a chuckle. It was her first date, so anything would have been the most romantic experience of her life. "He leaned in and just barely brushed his lips across mine. It was just like you described your first kiss with Papa."

"I'm happy for you, Elena." I hugged my daughter. "Now try to get some sleep. We have your grandmother's surgery in the morning." I turned out the lamp and closed my eyes.

"Momma... Thank you for being here tonight. I love you." Her words were so sweet.

"I love you, too. Goodnight."

A Second Offer

Bloody hell. I stood staring down into my mother-n-law's open abdomen. Dr. Flores, the general surgeon who assisted me, stood watching as I performed a complete hysterectomy. As I removed the ovaries, it was obvious that the cancer was at a very advanced stage. The organ tissue was discolored and full of small tumors protruding into the adjacent tissues. There was another larger tumor growing attached to her uterine wall. It was about the size of a navel orange with irregular borders and what seemed to be its own blood supply. I placed each organ in the large stainless steel bowl next to me. I looked at her liver and then up at Dr. Flores.

"The liver looks just as bad as her ovaries. You take a look and tell me if you think you can dissect out the tumors." I knew he would not be able to do it. There were too many and her liver looked rough and bumpy, like the liver of someone with irreversible cirrhosis. I watched as Dr. Flores looked inside her open abdominal cavity and examined the liver.

He raised his head, only our eyes were visible to each other due to our face masks. His eyes were all I needed to see to know that I was right. Her liver was beyond his ability to save it. I placed my hand inside of her body again and touched her liver. I was ready to begin the healing ritual.

I spoke the first few words to begin the prayer. An overwhelming oppressive feeling hit me. The pressure in the room built up around me and the temperature was rising. *Crap.* Death was here to warn me not to rid her liver of the tumors. It had allowed me the human rite to physically remove the other organs, but it was intervening now that I was invoking my healing powers.

"Everyone wait here. I'll be right back." I instructed the others assisting me. I walked to the window separating the waiting room from the scrub room. I turned on the intercom with my elbow so that her family could hear me.

"I've removed most of the diseased tissue." I paused, glad that they had insisted on leaving Elena at home. "Her liver is too damaged for Dr. Flores to remove the tumors." I focused my eyes on Marco speaking directly to him. "I can't save her. I'll close her back up and when she's out of recovery you'll be able to take her home. I don't think she has more than a few days left to live." From the overpowering feeling of death still in the room, I hoped that I could get her closed up and back home before he took her soul. I turned back to the operating room.

"If you heal her, I'll set you free of your commitment to me." I turned to find Adriano's hand pressed against the glass window looking directly at me. His eyes bore into mine. The pain from the words I had just delivered running out as tears streaked down his face. He loved his mother more than he hated his brother. He was bribing me to save her. I was thankful that I still had my surgical mask on and that none of them could see anything but my eyes. I flashed them towards Marco. His face was expressionless.

He knew what I had told him about Death. He knew what chances I was taking with my own fate if I tampered with Death's plans for his mother's soul. My heart melted as I looked at him. I turned again this time making it all the way to her body.

Sweat dripped down my forehead at the oppressive heat that was bearing down on me. I looked around at the others. They seemed unaffected. I thought about lowering my hand back into her open body. My hand moved hovering over the open space as I thought about freeing myself to be with Marco. Then I saw it. The light flashed over her body and I knew it was too late. Her vital signs were still good, but it would not be for long. From my experience, she had no more than an hour. I guess I would not know if I really would have tempted fate by pulling her from Death's grasp. I looked up at Dr. Flores.

"Close her up please. I'm going to let the family in as soon as you're done with the sutures." He nodded and began his task. I walked back out into the prep room I was in before, this time removing my mask, gloves, and surgical gown. I stepped out into the waiting room. The family stood and waited for me to speak. I looked at all of them standing there waiting to hear that I had saved her. I made eye contact with Leonardo.

"I'm sorry, Sir, but there was nothing more I could do. My ability was not strong enough. She is not gone yet, but her death is near." The family gasped and his daughters began crying loudly. I did not feel it necessary to explain that her soul no longer occupied her body. It would not offer them any comfort. "As soon as Dr. Flores is done closing up her incision, you can all go in to be with her."

I turned to go out of the waiting room, out of the hospital. I wanted to be with Elena. Adriano's emotions were overtaken with grief. I felt the intense love he possessed for his mother, as well as, the abyss of sadness that he was plummeting down. I wanted to distance myself as far away from him as I could, hoping that the physical distance would lessen the intensity at which I felt his sorrow. The further I traveled from the hospital the more I realized that it was not working.

Elena was reading in the garden when I returned to their home. I sat next to her under the patio. I put my arm around her, wishing that I would have changed out of the dirty scrubs I was wearing.

"Is grandmother better?" she asked, as she realized I was next to her.

"I'm sorry, Elena." I shook my head. "You remember how I told you there were certain circumstances when it was forbidden for me to heal?"

"Yes." She began to cry. "Is she dead?" She sniffled as her nose began to run.

"I don't know." I shrugged. "She was still alive when I left. Would you like to see her?" She nodded through her tears. We took her father's car back to the hospital.

When we walked into the room, they were all standing around her grandmother's body crying. Adriano's eyes lifted and accused me with his powerful gaze. There was a new layer to his emotions—hatred. He was angry and he was directing it towards me. Elena pushed through her aunts and laid her head on the dead woman's chest. This was the woman who had probably been the closest thing she had to a mother growing up. I wanted to go to her and comfort her, but Adriano's anger had me frozen and scared to move a muscle. I looked at Marco pleading with my eyes for him to comfort our daughter. He moved toward her, lifting her from his mother's dead body. He tried soothing her, but she continued to cry uncontrollably.

Adriano grabbed me by the drawstrings of my scrub pants and pulled me out of the room.

"Is this some cruel revenge? I offered you your freedom and you still let her die." His jaw muscle flexed with his words.

"I told you… I was too late. I went back to try again but Death claimed her soul before I could even attempt it. I would never intentionally hurt you or anyone else that way." He could feel my emotions to and he knew I was not lying, but he did not look like he cared. His anger stifled me. I could feel it rolling around inside of him growing the longer he focused his attention on me.

"You had to know that there was a chance that I wouldn't be able to heal her. I told you that I would try. I never guaranteed success." I pleaded with him to stop these horrible emotions that he was using to cripple me mentally and emotionally.

"I will never release you now. You and Marco will never be together. I will never allow it."

"You would stay joined to a woman that you loathed?" I asked not believing he could stand to continue to be my husband with the intensity of disgust I knew he was feeling.

"I may never touch you again but neither will he." He spit the words as he pointed toward the room where Marco stood mourning their mother.

"We'll just see about that." I squinted my eyes at him and poked him in the chest with my pointer finger. I turned on my heel and out of the door. I was totally innocent and he was blaming me for trying to help his mother. There had to be another way out of this relationship. I may have to use my abilities. I would contact the spirits for help.

Formulating a Plan

I ran to the nearest café and hailed a cab. Adriano's grief was suffocating me. I knew that physical distance would not decrease it, but there had to be some other way. How in the world their species was able to handle this type of crippling effect of the shared emotions was beyond my ability to understand.

The cab driver would only take me to the edge of town. He dropped me off at the dirt path that lead to Zamora's village. The only person who I felt could help me was Zamora. She had to know how to help me.

I found myself running down the dirt path to Zamora's small house. As it came into view, I could see her opening the front door. She definitely had the power of foresight. She was waiting for me. In her hand was a glass filled with some orange colored liquid.

"Drink," was all she said as I approached her. She shoved the glass into my hand. I did not question her. I just drank the warm fruit juice.

"I need your help," I said as I wiped a drop of the sweet juice from my chin.

"Come. Sit," she said, motioning me to follow her inside.

I entered her dwelling and settled at her kitchen table. I watched as she locked the front door and lit several candles around the small one-room house.

"You have angered your mate?" she asked. "So I take it the potion was not successful."

"No, it worked on the girl, but the plan failed. That isn't why he is angry. I couldn't save his mother without angering Death."

"I see," she said simply and poured me more juice. "Drink, you'll need it for your quest."

So I drank.

"Are you Noni's chosen successor," I asked not sure why I wanted to know this at this time? The question came unbidden to my lips.

"No. The chosen one has not stepped forward to fill the role." She looked at me expectantly.

"Am I ..." I began to ask.

"That is up to you. The people will embrace you because your power exceeds the last Mae-de-Santo or as you call her— Noni. However, it is a decision that you can only make for yourself. You have neglected your full range of powers for many years. You are capable of much more than you know."

"Oh," was my only audible reaction, but on the inside I

was literally freaking out. I never imagined I was to be the next Umbanda High Priestess. Noni never told me that is was my path. Maybe she couldn't tell me. Zamora said it was something I had to choose.

"You need to consult Mae-de-Santo." She was referring to Noni. I wondered if Noni communicated with her regularly.

She prepared a place on the floor for me to meditate. I reclined and slowed my breathing falling into a deep trace finding that place between sleep and awake.

Noni's long black and silver hair was tied in two braids that hung down the center of her back. She was motioning towards me lifting her gaze to meet my eyes. Her eyes flashed an intense gray and she held out her hand motioning me forward. She embraced me as she always did. I felt her warmth just as if her body was alive again. I inhaled deeply her sweet fragrance, the scent of magic and healing powers. She handed me a cup with a warm purple liquid and motioned for me to drink. I sipped the tea and winced in reaction to the harsh bitter flavor.

"Yuck…what is this?" I peered at her over the tea cup.

"It's what you need to heal the jaguar man's mark." She handed me a handful of beautiful purple flowers. The centers of the flowers a stark white contrast to the luxurious purple petals.

"But Zamora said there was no other way to get rid of Marco's power over me." I placed the cup on the small wooden table next to me inside the vision.

"Who do you think he went to when he was looking for his

149

potion to enchant you? Don't trust her. She wants your powers."
She reached for my hand and squeezed it lovingly. She went on to
explain that all I needed to do was heal myself and drink the tea
made from the purple flowers. She taught me the spell for making
the tea. "You will have to search the rainforest for the flowers.
They grow on the trunks of trees on a vine that climbs up to the
canopy. The flower blooms at dawn. You must make the tea and
perform the spell. Your new mate must mark you within three days.
If he fails to do so, you will remain under the control of the other."

"I might need a little more help than that, Noni."

"I will send you a boy."

"Boy?" I asked. "Surely a man would be better suited to
this task."

"The boy will guide you. He knows the rainforest better
than men four-times his age," she said. She sounded confident in
his abilities. I had to trust her judgment.

"How will I pay him? I have no money." I had fled the Barnardos' plantation with no belongings.

"You have something much more valuable," she said.
"Something he will desire more than all the money in the world."

"What will he want in return?" I asked.

"You will see. Rest. Your mate won't find you here. Zamora
is scared of his anger. She has cast a protection spell for now, but
don't stay here longer than you have to. She will find a way to turn
the tables on you."

"Noni, why didn't you tell me about the Jaguar's?" I asked. She had told me all about my abilities and her magic, but never once did she mention the existence of the shape shifters.

"My sweet child, I thought it was best. Maybe I was wrong." And with that she was gone and I was awake.

I opened my eyes to find Zamora sitting in front of me in a trance of her own. What was she trying to do? I imagined it was not for my benefit after hearing Noni's warning.

I slowly and quietly stood and left her house before she could awaken to find me still in her presence.

I stepped out into the early afternoon and wondered where I would find the boy who was to be my guide. I knew Noni would send him to me. I just hoped it would be soon. I tried to think of the best place to go in order to be away from Zamora, as well as, hide from Adriano.

I crept through the long grass that grew on the side of the dirt path that led back into the town. I had to find a safe place to stay. I turned toward the marketplace. Once I was at the edge of the town I made my way toward the vendors. This place was always packed with people. There would be safety in numbers.

I wandered toward a vendor with beautiful jewelry on display. I stared down at the table. My mouth dropped open when I saw an exact replica of the necklace that Marco had given me so many years ago. I touched the smooth cold black stone in the center of the silver pendant.

"I made that one to match Elena's," a young male voice

said. My head snapped up and I was looking into the clear blue eyes of Elena's friend Fern. He looked out of place with his red hair. No one else here had hair that was such a strange shade of red.

"You must like her very much," I replied.

"Yes." He shuffled his feet and pushed his hands inside his pants pockets looking nervous.

"Fern, where did you find this stone?" I asked. I knew that the stone was important.

"I find all my stones in the rain forest. There is a waterfall and cave that has some interesting rocks. I go into the forest often looking for stones to make jewelry." I felt a nagging nudge in my brain as he explained how he spent a lot of time in the rainforest.

Bingo. The guide had to Fern.

"Have you ever seen a purple and white flower growing in the forest?" I asked.

"Yes, lots."

"The one I'm looking for has large purple petals and a white star in the middle of the flower. It only blooms in the morning," I clarified.

He nodded. "I've seen it once or twice. It is rare."

"Do you think you could help me find it?" I asked.

"Yes, but the rain forest is dangerous, Mrs. Barnardos."

"Don't worry about that Fern. I need the flower. I'm willing to risk my safety, but I don't have any money to pay a guide."

"That's okay, I'm glad to help. I need to go back and look for stones anyway," he waved off my concern over payment for his services.

I smiled at my young guide. Elena had good taste. This young man was not only handsome, but kind and generous.

"When do we leave?" I asked.

"Tomorrow morning," he said. I have to let my family know we are leaving.

"Fern, I know this is a big imposition, but do you think I could stay with your family tonight?"

"Sure," he answered. "Are you in trouble, Mrs. Barnardos?"

"Yes, don't tell anyone where I am … not even Elena."

He nodded in agreement.

Fern thought it was best if I hid in a small shed in the back of his family's home. He felt that if I was in trouble he did not want to risk his mother telling anyone I was in his house. I agreed. He dropped me off in the shed and came back later with a blanket and some food to hold me over till the morning.

While sleeping I dreamt of Elena. I decided to try something that Noni had taught me so long ago. Dream-walking. Noni would often visit me in my dreams before she died. It was the only way she could train me while we were apart.

I channeled my energy into a tight ball of light and sent it out to Elena. My light brought me to a dark garden with tall scented flowers that I recognized as exaggerations of the plants in the Barnardos' courtyard garden. I tip-toed quietly through the plants and peered around the corner. The cement bench was occupied by Elena and her dream version of Fern.

They were in an intimate embrace of a kiss. A kiss that was much deeper than the one she described to me after their date. It was really sweet to see her dreaming of him, but I needed to speak to her. I stepped out of the foliage and onto the paved pathway.

"Elena, I need to speak to you," I interrupted. She looked up at me and the dream version of Fern vanished into the mist of the garden.

"Momma," she said surprised.

"Listen, I must tell you something. I don't know how long I can maintain my presence here in your dream."

"You're really in my dream? I'm not just dreaming about you?" she asked.

"No, you aren't just dreaming." I shook my head. "I'm dream-walking."

"Is that dangerous?" she asked.

"No, if you wake up my energy just snaps back to my body," I explained.

"Cool. I have the coolest mother ever," she said proudly.

"I'm going on a little trip to find something that will allow your father and I to be together. I don't know how long it will take, but I will be back. Please tell him, but don't say anything to your uncle. Do you understand?" I asked.

"Yes, but why don't you just tell him yourself?" she asked.

"What do you mean?"

"Duh, dream walk inside his head, Momma." She looked at me with that expression that teenagers the world over have perfected. The look that says my parents are total morons. I went from the coolest mom ever to moron mom.

"Oh, you think he'd be alright with that?" I asked.

"Really, Momma. Go ahead. He loves you."

"Okay," I agreed. "Elena …"

"Yes, Momma?"

"I'm sorry I interrupted your dream of Fern. I really do like him. He is such a nice young man."

"It's okay. He's still here," she explained pointing towards a dark shadow hiding behind a palm frond. I waved at him and he waved back smiling.

Young love is so sweet.

I pulled back my energy searching out dream waves in the house. There was a powerful one emanating close by, but it felt dark. It was a nightmare and I did not want any part of a nightmare. I continued to feel out other dream waves.

"Bingo," I said to no one in particular, as I wrapped my energy into a dream that I was sure belonged to Marco.

Blue-green waves crashed against pure white sand and the sounds of sunset were all around. De ja vu hit me. I had been here before. I found an abandoned beach umbrella and sat beneath it to hide. The only thing different about my visit to this beach, and this dream, was that there were more people in my real experience. This beach was deserted, except for one young couple.

Three umbrella's down was a young man and woman. They were wrapped in each other. This jumble of arms and legs was the younger version of Marco and me, one being locked together so tightly that nothing could exist outside of us.

I remembered that feeling like it was yesterday. When we were together it felt like there was only us. We were in our own perfect world.

This younger dream version of me wiggled away from the younger Marco and ran into the ocean. He watched her for a long moment, smiling at her with such intense admiration. It touched my heart seeing the expression on his face.

He stood and followed her into the ocean. I relived this vision of my past by watching them play in the warm water with the sunset turning into night. This part of my past was what I had longed for over the years of separation. This was my one perfect summer.

Then suddenly the scenery shifted, I found myself sitting in the corner of Marco's bedroom. On the bed was the older more mature current day Marco and he was holding his dream version of the current day me. I watched as the two of them writhed between the sheets locked in a moment of passion.

I sat there, quiet, watching them. This was wrong. Even though I was technically watching myself make love, I still felt as if I was witnessing something private. I felt guilty being there. However, I could not bring myself to interrupt this moment. It was the only way we could be together until we were rid of Adriano's mark. I did not want to take this dream away from Marco.

I wondered if I did interrupt and took the place of the dream version of me if that would technically break my vow to Adriano. I was not sure what would happen so I just could not take the chance.

I slipped out of his dream, leaving him, and holding onto the happy memories of our times together. I had to find those purple flowers and get back in time to save our only chance for true happiness.

On my way back through the dream waves, I felt an intense pull toward the dark dream that I had avoided before. I decided to allow the nightmare to pull me in.

I found myself in the middle of the rainforest. A feeling of intense sexual need taking over my body, the sensation was so strong, I couldn't differentiate if it was my own or that of my mate. My entire body was on fire with desire. I stretched and allowed the lovely ache to spread out over my body. I inhaled deeply enjoying the scent of my mate. My mind struggled against the physical desire that my body obviously could not fight.

"So glad you could join me, Gatinho?" Adriano's deep rumbling voice rolled through my brain and enveloped all my nerve endings in a wonderful softness. My eyes focused on my surroundings. The thick foliage of the rainforest blocked out all light. All I could see with my weak human vision was the two glowing copper eyes staring at me in between the branches and leaves.

"What are you doing here?" I asked, backing away from the glowing eyes right up against a tree trunk. Adriano stepped forward close enough for me to see his smiling face. "I thought you were mad at me for letting your mother die?"

He frowned at the reminder of his mother's death. "I am angry with you, but I also miss you." He moved his hand down the length of my arm. "I couldn't stand to be separated from you any longer." He leaned down to kiss my lips.

"Adriano." I turned to avoid the temptation of his lips. "I don't think we should…"

"Gathino," he interrupted. "I know you can feel how badly I need you. I've put up with your neglect for long enough. It is unnatural that you continue to deny me my most basic of husbandly rights." He released that low guttural noise deep in his chest as he rubbed his face along my cheek. The stubble from his lack of shaving was long enough that it did not prickle my skin. It was actually soft and felt wonderful.

"Can you feel what I've been feeling?" I asked as he nuz-

zled my neck, kissing his way down to my collarbone.

"Yes, I know you're feeling guilty and you're sorry." He pulled the straps of my nightgown down over my shoulders. Wow, in the previous dreams I had just been in jeans and a t-shirt. Somehow I've become incorporated into his actual dream.

"I understand that if you would have saved her it would have meant horrible things for you. It just took me a little while to come to terms with it," he continued. This dream version of Adriano wanted to make-up.

"You were willing to let me go to save her and now you just expect me to sleep with you?" I tried to give him my best look of righteous indignation. "Of all the nerve… you…you told me you loved me. You lied. You beast!" My hands fisted in his open shirt. He didn't react to my tirade just continued to kiss and lick his way down my neck. "Adriano!" I screamed as I smacked the back of his head. "Stop it."

"Alright, but I didn't lie. I do love you, not the way Marco does, but I do love you." He waggled his thick almost black eye brows at me. "You are still mine. We are bound and I'm not letting you go, so it is your duty to satisfy my needs."

"What cave did you crawl out of?" I just shook my head in disbelief at his level of nerve.

"Gatinho, you had your chance to be with him and you choose not to take it."

"You're wrong, I was going to save her, but death swooped in and grabbed her soul before I could interfere. I hesitated just a moment thinking about what it would mean to do it, the years it would have taken off my own life. I would have given up those years to be with Marco, but death didn't allow me the chance." I lowered my head onto his chest.

"I see," he said, before chewing on the inside of his cheek. I felt the sadness as he realized that what I was saying was true. He could feel my emotions just as strongly as I could feel his. He knew that I did not want him. I was rejecting him in favor of his brother. The sadness grew and altered into hatred. The hatred he felt for Marco deepening and opening up fresh wounds. "Why does everyone always choose him?" He so obviously wanted to be loved. I honestly felt sorry for him. He had deep emotional childhood issues that I did not fully understand.

"Don't you think you're being a little narcissistic?" I put my hand under his chin. "Everyone doesn't choose Marco. You're just seeing it that way because you're focusing on the relationships that he has with the people in his life. I was a part of his life before you ever knew me. He is your oldest brother, so it is natural that you feel that your parents loved him more. Every child feels that way about his siblings. What about Luciana I know you still have feelings for her?"

"What are you a psychiatrist, now? Thank you for that analysis, but you really have no clue what you are talking about." He wrapped his arms around me and kissed me hard on the mouth. His lips forcefully parting mine as he pushed his tongue into my mouth. His mouth had no mercy with this kiss and his emotions matched the hardness of his body. I knew what he was thinking without him having to say anything out loud. He was letting me

know that he would never let me go. What he did not know was that I had a way out now thanks to Noni's advice.

I had to find a way out of this dream. I didn't want to make love to him, even in a dream. Which was funny, because before we had left for Las Vegas I had dreamt of making love to him many times.

"Adriano, what really happened between you and Marco?" I asked. "Is it really just about you wanting to run the family business?"

"Of course that is what this whole business between the three of us is about," he said.

He was lying. He knew that I knew he was lying. His desire to be in charge of the business was part of his reason for bringing me into the family. He did want me to provide him with a child and he wanted to emotionally hurt his brother. Something had happened between them that no one was telling me.

"What has he done to you?" I asked Adriano as I thought about Marco. I loved him, but I was realistic. I knew that it was possible that Marco had done something horrible to cause this rift between the two brothers. "I know that there is something that happened that you are both leaving out. It is not fair for you to torture me for your brother's sins against you. I deserve to know why you have bound me to you." He did not speak. I was determined to get the answer, so I just waited patiently for him to make the decision to tell me.

Suddenly, I was filled with a renewed desire for Marco. I imagined myself leaning across the floor of his limo and grabbing his face and just kissing him into a frenzied passion. My heart beat sped up and my body responded to the nature of my mind's lascivious thoughts. I was so wrapped up in the thought of touching and kissing Marco that I did not hear Adriano speaking right away. He shook me. I felt his jealousy and anger rage inside of him. I realized I was having a vision. A vision of what was wrong between the two men.

"He slept with her didn't he?" I asked the dream version of my mate. "That is what drove you to seek me out. You are using me to punish him because he seduced the woman you love." He did not answer me right away. "Was it Luciana?"

Before I could get an answer from him, I found myself back inside my body in the small dank shed behind Fern's home. Adriano must have woken up. Well that would not do. I needed to know the answer. I closed my eyes and sent my energy back out to the Barnardos' plantation. This time I recognized which dream vibrations were Marco's and didn't bother tip toeing inside his head.

"I want the truth," I said.

The dream version of myself disappeared as Marco focused on me standing at the foot of his bed. He rubbed his eyes. "You are still dreaming," I said, explaining the whole dream walking concept.

"Have you ever done that to me before?" he asked.

"Earlier tonight. I watched you make love to me. It was an interesting experience," I smiled.

He smiled back.

"We could do it again if you like," he offered. I moved closer to him wishing I could take him up on the offer, but my intuition told me that I shouldn't. It would break my vow to Adriano and give him the right to kill Marco. I wanted to know everything that went on to make Adriano so miserable.

"I want you to tell me what happened between you and Luciana," I said softly as I placed my hand on his bare chest.

"Do I really have to discuss this with you?" he asked. "You should have asked Adriano to explain it."

"He was telling me, but he woke up from his dream before he could finish."

"I am a man. I may still love you, but I have physical needs." I nodded in agreement, hoping he would elaborate. "I've never found another woman who made me feel the way that you do, but that doesn't mean that I didn't look for one who could."

"I understand." And the truth was that I really did understand. We had been apart for so long; it would have been unreasonable to expect that he never enjoyed the company of other women or attempted to find love. "I'll be honest. I'm shocked that you never married."

"I was engaged once." He admitted…fidgeting with the edge of the soft bed sheets. "But it didn't work out."

"Why not?"

"It was an arranged engagement. She was the eldest daughter of another jaguar family. I didn't love her and when she started making demands that I send Elena away to boarding school …," he shook his head in disgust. "I refused her request. We mutually agreed that it wouldn't work."

"Well, I was engaged, too." I offered to make him feel better about his admission of his previous relationships.

"I am aware of Rhett," he said. "I was happy with your choice in him. I wanted you to be happy, Biddy. I felt that he was good for you."

"Let's get something straight," I wagged my finger at him. "You are the only man that could possibly make me happy." The red birthmark on his face darkened. I had almost forgotten how it would always give his feelings away. Before I could react he was on me. His mouth on mine. His lips teasing and taunting me to open to his desire to show me the depths of what he was feeling after my declaration that he was the only man on earth who could make me happy. I allowed myself to melt against him and feel the relief and happiness of being in his arms again. "Stop…wait," I gasped between kisses as I reluctantly pushed him away. "Adriano…he…"

"He what?" Marco interrupted, distancing himself from me, waiting for me to answer. I touched my swollen lips and tried to temper my emotions.

"I need to know why he hates you. Let's get back to the story. What happened with Luciano?" I asked. "She can shift right?" I knew this because of her eyes.

"Yes," he nodded. "Her people live deep in the rain forest,

but she came here to attend school." He went on to explain that Adriano and Luciana had met in school and they had been inseparable. Even though Adriano didn't confide his feelings to Marco, it was obvious to him that his little brother was in love. His sisters told him that Adriano was planning on proposing to Luciana and that he had asked her father's blessing.

"So what went wrong?"

"She went into heat." He didn't voluntarily offer more information. He just watched me.

"What?" I asked as I gave him my best confused shrug.

"When an unmarked female of our species goes into heat it is a precarious situation." He leaned back and watched me.

"Why?" I asked.

"Because every unmated male will desire her. She is vulnerable to unsolicited attention. Her scent, her movements, and even her behavior will taunt the males. She is at the height of her desirability. She is fertile." Great, as if I didn't feel inadequate enough, now there was this other mysterious mating fertility thing that I could not offer him. "Unmated males will compete for her attention and the right to claim her during her fertile time. You know this is actually one thing that I'm happy I never had to worry about with you. It's hard enough just having men ogling your woman, but this is even harder."

"So you slept with her while she was in heat?" I was relieved that he did not feel like something had been missing from our relationship.

"No, he thinks I did, but…," he shook his head. The sheet slipped down and I caught sight of his stomach and hip.

"So why did he seek revenge on you?" I asked, trying to push down my lusty thoughts.

"Because, there were a group of us who competed for the right to have her," he explained. The way he said it, so nonchalantly, bothered me. It was as if it was perfectly natural for a woman to be the center of a brutal physical fight.

"What?" I imagined that the look on my face was at this point totally flabbergasted.

"The female goes through this time in our jaguar form. The males fight for the right to take her."

"And she goes along with this?" I asked confused again. "She enjoys this?"

"Yes, it is primal to us. That day there were five or six of us in our jaguar forms fighting over her." It was starting to make sense to me. "So if you didn't win and I assume Adriano didn't win…who did?"

"Our cousin, Jose. He is much stronger and bigger than the rest of us."

"So why is he mad at you?"

"Because I didn't support his desire to kill Jose," he paused, "and of course because I beat him in the challenge. The final fight for Luciana was between Jose and me."

"But I thought you agreed that Adriano was stronger and faster than you?"

"He is without a doubt, but I told you, I'm smarter. Adriano is led only by his emotions. He doesn't keep his head in the fight."

"So did Jose mark Luciana?" I asked.

"No, Adriano knocked him off her before it got that far. She did get pregnant, but she lost the baby."

"So Adriano wouldn't take her back?"

"No…he felt that she betrayed him…that we all betrayed him."

"Why didn't he mark her?" If they were lovers it would have made sense that he would have marked her especially when he planned on marrying her.

"They were waiting for their official wedding."

"He is romantic," I admitted.

"You realize he is just using you right," he replied to my comment about Adriano's romantic nature with a twinge of jealousy in his tone.

"I know…" I smiled at him. "I'm just saying he has a seriously thick romantic streak…"

"I really don't want to hear about anything thick that my brother possesses," he interrupted.

"You really need to remove your mind from the gutter.

That's not what I was talking about. You know that I love you and that I want to be with you." The look on his face was hard to read. "You do know that don't you?"

"I love you, too. It's just hard for me to see you in his arms." He ran his hand through is black hair and scratched the back of his head, as he watched me pace in front of him.

"I understand and I' m sorry. I wish I was stronger." He reached out and grabbed my waist pulling me into him. "I've found a way for us to be together."

"How?" His eyebrows crinkled together in disbelief.

"There is a purple flower that grows on a vine that climbs up the trunk of the trees in the canopy of the rain forest. The flower has a white star in the center."

He nodded.

"Do you know it?" I asked, hoping that he knew exactly where we could find one of the plants.

"Yes, but it is rare. The flower only blooms at dawn. The vine has very few leaves so it is hard to find during the day." He paused as he drew me closer to him. "What does the flower do?"

I told him about my vision of Noni and the spell she taught me to make the potion from the flowers.

"If I drink the potion then his mark will disappear. He will have no hold on me. My bond to him will be broken." A slow smile spread across his face as I spoke about being free from his brother.

"I can you find these flowers for you."

"No. I have to do it. That is part of the magic. I must be the one to pick the flowers."

"I'll guide you."

"No," I said. "I already have a guide. I must do this without you. But once I drink the potion you have three days to mark me. You have to know that this is what you want. If you don't mark me within that time then I revert back to Adriano's mate."

"I'll find you. I promise."

A Quest with Fern

$\mathcal{I}$ was already awake when Fern entered the shed with some breakfast for me. He was carrying a backpack of supplies for our adventure. We stepped out into the dark morning.

"How long will it take us to get there?" I asked my young companion.

"The waterfall is at least a two hour journey. I have a trail that I can drive my jeep through for the first hour, but then we will be on foot."

"Okay, I can handle that," I said confidently. "Your parents are okay with you trekking through the rainforest alone?"

"My mother doesn't like it, but ever since my father's illness, they really have no choice. We have to have the stones to make the jewelry."

"What type of injury?" I asked.

"Crippling arthritis in his hands and his legs." Fern went on to explain how his mother and father worked together to make the jewelry their family sold in the market. It was his mother's family who were the metal and stone jewelry makers. His father learned the craft from his mother when they first married. His mother was the real artist and Fern's father was the one who went on the expeditions to locate the stones for the jewelry. He taught Fern everything he knew about locating the colorful rocks. So his mother could still make jewelry but she had to rely on Fern searching for the stones when he was out of school.

I reached beneath my shirt collar and wrapped my fingers around the simple black pendant that Marco had given me so long ago.

"Can I see that?" he asked, pointing to my necklace.

"Sure," I said, releasing the pendant to allow it to lay flat above my shirt.

"That's Elena's necklace," he said. "She wore it at the dance."

"I let her borrow it. Her father gave it to me when I was her age," I explained.

"My mother is a wonderful craftsman. Even back then her work was unbelievable."

"Fern, when we return, I'd like to examine your father. Maybe I can help." This must have been what Noni was referring to when she said that I possessed something my guide would value more than money.

"I thought you were a lady doctor? You know that you delivered babies," he said blushing a little at the thought of what my job entailed.

"Yes, but maybe I can help your father," I explained.

"I would like that. It would make life for my mother better," he answered.

We've been walking for over two hours since Fern parked his jeep at the end of a forest trail. He was leading the way, often turning to check on how I was handling our trek through the rainforest. I could tell that I was slowing him down.

I smiled, as I watched him cutting vines and branches, in order to create a path for me. Pride filled me as I watched him. My daughter had made a good choice in choosing him. This young man was not only handsome, but also artistic and caring. He reminded me of her father.

"It's not much further. Listen," he said, cupping his hand around his ear. "Can you hear the waterfall?" His other hand held a branch above my head.

"Yes, I hear it." The sound of the water fall, and the knowledge that Fern had seen the purple flowers in this area, increased my stamina. I suddenly found renewed energy to keep going.

"It'll be getting dark soon," he said.

"Fern, it's already dark." This far into the rainforest there was not much sunlight breaking through the tree canopy.

"I mean nighttime dark. We have to make camp soon."

"Where?" I asked. I've never been a camping type of person.

"The flowers bloom early in the morning. So we will sleep in the cave behind the waterfall and set an alarm to wake us up early."

"I don't know a lot about the rainforest, but don't animals sleep in caves? Like big hungry cats?"

"You've been in the dean of the rainforest's most dangerous cats. Believe me this cave is much safer."

"What?" My mouth fell open. What did Fern know about the Barnardos family.

He laughed. I guess my reaction was funny to him. I just continued to stare at him.

"I am Curupira and a follower of Umbanda. Zamora is our priestess, but we all have been waiting for you. There are prophecies about the great high priestess who will come to help her people and end the control of the Jaguars. I believe you are the new Mae-de-Santo."

I shook my head.

"I can't fill my great-grandmother's shoes."

"You can and you will. She foretold it herself," he explained.

"Wait! You knew about my daughter's family and you still wanted to take her out. That was brave." I looked at Fern with even more admiration.

"Or stupid, but love will make you do stupid things."

We were now at the mouth of the cave on the back side of the waterfall. He removed his back pack and began setting up a fire to cook the food rations his mother had prepared.

"Tell me more about the jaguar people." I said, as we ate. My great-grandmother had not left me with any knowledge of them. Of course, I now knew much more than I ever really wanted to know, but if I was going to be successful at breaking my mate's hold then it was imperative that I know more.

"You know the bulk of it," he started. "The only thing that you may not fully understand is that the Barnardos family are tyrants who imprison the local people with their drug trafficking. The locals are too scared of the legend to go against Mr. Barnardos and his sons. So much so that the Barnardos men haven't actually had to enforce any disciplinary actions for decades. Old man Barnardos was quite the terror when he was younger."

I knew this to be true because of Adriano's admission that his father and mother's relationship was abusive at times and that his father often turned an abusive hand on his younger son out of anger. It was one of his motivating factors for seeking me out in the first place.

"What about Elena's father?" I asked.

"To be honest, all the villagers just assume he's as hard as his father. He's never really done anything to show that he actually is. I guess his father's reputation was bad enough to carry over to his sons needlessly.

"Maybe not," I said, thinking of everything that Adriano had done to use me against his brother. There was more I wanted to ask Fern, but I was tired from the long journey and fell asleep before I could ask.

"Wake up, Mrs. Barnardos or should I call you Mae-de-Santo?" Fern asked, as he shook my shoulder gently.

I opened my eyes and looked around the cave. My night's sleep had been restful. I awoke with a renewed hope at finding the elusive purple flowers. It must have been the sound of the roaring waterfall that had supplied me with such restful sleep.

"I feel so rested. Sleeping in the cave was a great idea. Did you get any sleep? I asked my brave guide.

"No, but I'll sleep tonight after we have found the flowers. I was awake because a jaguar tracked us, but I was able to lead him away from you."

"How? Who?" I asked.

"It's one of my talents. Didn't Noni ever tell you about the Curupira?" he asked, running his hand through his spiky red hair.

"She told me that they were little red headed fairies with backwards feet," I answered, looking down at his feet. Which I was glad to see were facing the right direction. He laughed before offering to take off his hiking boots to prove his toes pointed forward.

"No, that is the legend, but my magic deals more with protecting the forest and its animals." He went on to explain how he can trick hunters or anyone who isn't playing fairly in their hunt.

He could mimic animal sounds and call upon the forest's creatures to help him.

"So, did Marco know who you were?" I asked.

"Yes," Fern chuckled. "I think that's the only reason I made it out the door with Elena. He knew I would and could protect her."

After cleaning up our camping gear, Fern and I set off for the peak of the mountain. It was still dark but Fern lit the way with a headlamp, and I carried a slender black flashlight. The animals of the rainforest filled the air with sound as we rustled through the foliage. I felt safe with Fern, especially knowing about his special gifts. We walked in silence, listening to the animals around us talking. Every now and then Fern would mimic the sounds of the birds or a monkey. I didn't question him, but I assumed he was communicating with them. I started to think of him as my own Doctor Doolittle.

"We'll stop here. I'm sure we will find your flowers bloom-ing in this area," he said. He was so confident that I believed we would, too. I nodded in agreement and took the heavy backpack off my shoulders, rolling my neck in relief. Fern also lowered his pack to the ground then sat on it. I followed his example.

It wasn't long before the sun started to rise. As the sunlight hit the dewy leaves of the plants, my mouth fell open at the beauty surrounding us. There were mountains in the distance and colorful birds singing concordant melodies. The sounds seemed to be wel-coming the new day. I looked around but I didn't see any purple flowers with white star centers. I looked at Fern and he shook his head. He pulled a pair of binoculars from a side zippered pocket of his backpack and held them to his eyes surveying the surrounding area.

I decided to wander around looking for the flowers on my own. I could hear a low rumbling sound, something that I knew I had heard before. It was deep and calming, like it was luring me closer. The low vibratory murmur called to me … drawing me into its seductive tone. I could feel it in my bones. I looked around for its source and decided that it was coming from the top of a nearby rock formation. The sound grew louder as I walked closer. I lifted a large palm frond and the sound stopped. The silence brought on a feeling of emptiness.

I looked around the rock formation to find what animal was making that wonderful sound. No matter how hard I looked I couldn't find any animals, but what I did find was a vine with clusters of purple flowers with white star centers.

"Fern!" I called out. "Over here. I've found them." I was jumping up and down in place, so excited with my find that I forgot about the animalistic melody that had drawn me to the spot for a moment, but then out of the corner of my eye I saw a flash of movement.

Fern came running over. He found me sitting next to the vine. I was wondering what was the best way to preserve the flowers. I didn't have much time. Once picked the flowers needed to be mixed quickly into the potion. Flowers as delicate as these wouldn't last long separated from their source of nourishment.

I rubbed the petals gently between my thumbs and forefingers. The purple petals were silky smooth. I leaned in closer to the flower and inhaled its strong perfume. With my eyes closed, I drew its fragrance deep into my lungs. The scent pulled on a memory of Noni dressed in her long white robes standing in front of the fire pit at the center of her village. The sparks from the fire floating in the air around her like fireflies. She commanded the sparks with an incantation to prophesy. The sparks flashed bright around her twirling swirling in a dizzying vision. Her arms dropped to her sides and then standing there in those white robes was no longer Noni, but me. My hair was wild and windblown.

"Why didn't you tell me?" I asked my great-grandmother. Even though she wasn't in my line of sight, I knew her ethereal spirit was still present.

"You weren't ready. You were getting closer to unleashing your full potential, but then your heart was broken. That stunted your ability to fully accept the weight of your powers." Noni's disembodied voice filled my mind.

"So now that I've found my love I'm ready," I said guessing.

"No. It was never about him. You were missing the confidence you needed."

"Mrs. Barnardos," Fern said, shaking my shoulder. "What's wrong?"

"Just a vision." I shook my head clearing the foggy feeling from my brain. My eyes felt heavy.

"Are you ready to get started?" he asked.

I wondered if he could sense the animal that led me to the flowers. He seemed nervous. His eyes scanned the area surrounding us. I opened my backpack and pulled out a bottle of Carpirinha, a Brazilian Rum, and poured some into an empty water bottle. I pulled five of the purple flowers from the vine, breaking them into pieces. Then I pushed the crushed petals inside the water bottle to mix with the rum.

"Why'd you need the rum?" he asked. I had given him a list of items I needed and he had to take the rum from his parents' liquor cabinet.

"The alcohol will help break down the chemicals inside the petals faster than if I mixed them with plain water," I explained.

I shook the bottle and the mixture turned a beautiful deep purple. I did not tell Fern, but I had also selected the rum hoping it would improve the taste of the concoction. If it tasted as bitter as it had in my dream it would be difficult to keep it down.

"I'm not sure what will happen after I drink this. Just promise you won't leave me here alone."

"I promise. Elena would never forgive me if anything happened to you. She is so happy that you have found each other." I closed my eyes and raised the bottle above my head.

"Great Olorum, bless your daughter in her quest for cleansing. Send Xango to bring me justice after years of separation from my lover and my child. Send Omolu to provide health and healing of this jaguar's mark." I drank the entire contents of the bottle. The sugar in the rum improved the taste slightly, but it was still bitter. I chased the potion with a swig straight from the bottle of Carpirinha.

Clouds moved over us and lightening was followed by a loud clap of thunder.

"Let's get back to our cave," Fern said as he lifted me to my feet. The forest was quiet except for the rain and thunder. My mind was quiet as well. I could feel myself smiling. Adriano's emotions were gone. I had forgotten how nice it was not to have someone else sharing my every emotion. It felt light and almost empty, but a good empty. I realized how much of my feelings I was holding back in order to not share them with Adriano.

I followed Fern as he half walked half jogged down the trail toward the cave. As soon as we made it to the shelter I was going to put my backpack down and feel my shoulder for the scar.

By the time we made it back to the cave the rain was coming down in sheets through the thick leaves of the trees. Fern stopped just outside of the cave. He leaned in close and whispered something into my ear, but I couldn't hear him over the sound of the heavy rain.

"What?" I asked.

He wiped the rain from his face.

"Something's in the cave," he said louder.

"What is it?" I asked, blinking away the drops of rain collecting in my eyelashes.

"I can't tell. The rain is throwing off my radar. I just know it's an animal."

"It must be Marco. He said he would find me." He was here to mark me, to claim me. My heart was beating faster at the thought of finally being with Marco after all these years. We could be a family now. I rushed past Fern into the dark cave.

"Wait, let me go first," he shouted. But it was too late. I was already inside the cave. I stopped short and felt Fern run into my back.

A large black jaguar was pacing back and forth. The only thing I knew for sure was that it wasn't Adriano.

Adriano was the only jaguar shifter that I had seen shift frequently. This cat was a little smaller than Adriano. The only time I had ever seen Marco in their alternate form was in the dark when I was half asleep. He did tell me that his younger brother was bigger than him so this jaguar could easily be Marco or it could be a real jaguar upset that we were using his home for our camp.

Fern moved to stand in front of me. We both knew that if it was a real jaguar he could protect me.

"Marco?" I asked, peaking around Fern's shoulder.

The jaguar stopped pacing and stared at us.

"Marco, I'm free. You need to mark me before your brother wakes up and realizes what I've done."

Fern and I watched as the jaguar shifted into his human form. The process fascinated me no matter how many times I witnessed it.

"Mr. Barnardos, what are you doing here, sir?" The jaguar

turned out to be Marco's father.

Fern grabbed some shorts from his bag and handed them to the eldest Barnardos male, who looked like he was still in great shape for a man his age. I was starting to think that the feline DNA had something to do their ability to maintain their physiques.

"I'm here to accomplish something neither of my sons could do," Leonardo said, as he pulled the shorts on and thanked Fern.

"What might that be?" I asked.

"You are going to give this family the child that we want," he explained.

"You have got to be kidding me." He was expecting me to have a baby with him. That wasn't going to be happening.

"Do I look like I'm joking?"

"With all due respect, I'm not having a child with you." I folded my arms over my chest and starred back at Leonardo.

"You don't really have a choice in the matter, Gatinho."

"Oh, no you don't. There is only one man who can call me that and it's not you. Besides, Marco is out looking for me now. Don't you think he'll be upset if you rape me?" I asked.

"I won't rape you, my dear. You'll succumb willingly. You'll be begging for it," he said with an evil sneer taking over his smile.

"How do you see that playing out?" I asked.

"First, I'm going to mark you." Adriano must not have told his father that I was able to withstand the effects of the jaguar mark. I wasn't going to give that bit of information away, either. Leonardo moved closer to me, ready to mark me as his mate. "Thank you for allowing my wife to die. I couldn't have even thought about doing this if she had survived. I'll even let you decide where you want the mark."

"How generous of you," I said. The sarcasm in my tone was obvious. I looked over at Fern trying to signal him for help or an idea of how to get out of this situation. He mouthed something that I couldn't understand. I shrugged, as Leonardo Barnardos stood only inches away from me.

"You can never send a boy to do a man's job," he stated before grabbing my arm. The old man was strong.

"Let go of her!" Fern shouted, moving to my side and trying to release me from Leonardo's grasp. The old man's free hand reared back and knocked Fern to the ground. The sound of Fern's head hitting the cave floor did not bode well for Fern. Neither did the pool of bright red blood forming around his head. I just hoped he could hang on long enough for me to figure out a way to free myself to heal his injury.

"Stop! I'll agree to the marking if you let me heal the boy," I said, bargaining with the evil old man.

"Marking first," he said and before I could say anything else he lifted my arm and bit.

"Let me go so I can heal the boy," I screamed as I watched his teeth sinking into my skin.

"Maybe I shouldn't. He is useless to me." My new mate growled with my blood fresh on his lips.

"Your granddaughter is in love with him."

"She is useless to me as well," he stated, flatly.

"How dare you speak about my daughter that way." I lifted my good arm to swing it towards his head. He caught it and held me by both arms.

"You are my mate now and that means you will do as I say," he said through gritted teeth.

"Never! I was marked as a mate before and didn't do what he wanted. What makes you think I'll listen to you?" I asked. "I've already told you, I need to heal the boy. You either let me or I will refuse anything else you ask of me."

He released my wrists, finally seeing that he was not dealing with his fragile wife. I turned to Fern and dropped to my knees to assess the damage to his skull. His breathing was shallow and his pulse was weak.

"Go now and get help," I shouted. My new mate looked at me shaking his head 'no.'

"Fine." I placed my hands over Fern's head and began to chant. I could hear Leonardo moving to reform the small fire Fern had made the night before at the entrance to the cave. I didn't know why he was doing it, but I hoped the smoke would help either Adriano or Marco to find us. The heavy rain had lightened up, but it had probably also cleaned out any trail we left behind on our morning hike.

I looked down at Fern as I prayed, but my powers did not seem to be working. He was still bleeding. Head wounds were notorious for producing lots of blood. I continued to chant but also now tried to physically stop the bleeding. I wrapped a t-shirt around his head.

I flexed my fingers back over Fern and began chanting again. The temperature surrounding me rose. I opened my eyes to see if Leonardo had lit the fire, but he was still trying to get it started. That could only mean one thing. Death was here for Fern.

No. I couldn't let this generous young man die. I wanted my daughter to have a happy life from now on. If she was in love with Fern then they deserved a shot at happiness. Without even thinking about it I extended my body over him instinctively trapping his soul in my magic. I changed my chant to include a protection from death spell. I tried not to think about what I was going to have to give up. The temperature around me rose even higher. I could feel the sweat building up and dripping off my body. Heaviness settled on top of me. The weight of death was upon me, not only my body where I could feel the physical heaviness, but also an emotional torment that racked my brain. Then it hit me like lightening. Death was trying to decide what to take from me. It was searching my mind to find something I held valuable. I shut out all thoughts of Marco and Elaina. I mentally locked the memories of them inside my mind. Then I dared to speak to death directly.

"A mate for a mate." I filled my head with the image of Leonardo biting my arm. I let death see the mental and emotional connection that I now shared with my mate. "It's only fair. Take my mate in place of another's." I dared not even speak her name.

"Why?" Death asked inside my brain.

"Because he took this boy's life before it was time," I answered.

"I decide when it's time," Death answered.

"I've never asked this of you before, when all along I could have. I have great respect for you."

"No, my daughter what you have is fear."

"Does that please you?" I asked.

"Yes, but the jaguar is not injured. He must at least be injured."

I tried to figure out a way to hurt Leonardo, but I did not want to leave Fern's soul vulnerable to Death. If I moved the protection spell would disappear.

"How much longer is this going to take? I'm ready to get you home," Leonardo asked. His voice sounded bored. I was stuck unable to stop my protection prayers and unable to injure Leonardo. I continued my chanting trying to figure out what to do next.

"We need to go. My son is near. I can sense him, " Leonardo said as he paced near the fire.

Good. Marco would be able to help me.

Leonardo reached down to move me away from Fern. I struggled to remain over Fern's body. The bleeding had stopped

and his breathing was getting stronger, but I knew if I gave up even for a second Death would take him.

I heard the angry chortle of a big cat behind me. His heavy paws were silent against the cave floor but he was moving closer. He nuzzled my shoulder and released a deep growl in his chest. I knew he could sense the change in me. I had been marked by Leonardo.

The jaguar turned to Leonardo and stalked forward with slow deliberate steps. His head held low and even with his shoulders ... ready to strike. Leonardo fazed back into his cat form and the two jaguars began circling each other.

I continued to chant while I watched the two large cats continue their slow dance. I knew the smaller cat was Leonardo, but I also knew that his size was not a good indicator of his strength. Leonardo took the first aggressive strike, biting Marco on the shoulder. I knew the main objective of this fight was for one of them to bite the others throat causing a puncture wound that would kill the other. All I needed was for Leonardo to at least be injured and Death would take my bargain.

The two fought by swiping their giant paws at each other always circling trying to find a weakness in their opponent.

The oppressive heat of Death was wearing me down, as I was watching the two cats fight. I decided I had to do something different. I changed my chant to that of a protection spell for Marco ... asking the spirits to protect him during the fight. Then I yelled out to him.

"Injure him, my love. It is the only way." I knew Marco

would not want to kill his father. I on the other head had no qualms about handing the evil man over to Death. "Hurt him," I yelled again.

The bigger jaguar crouched low and sprang at his father grabbing him by the neck and started to shake his head back and forth. The smaller jaguar was pinned to the ground. A pool of his blood started to gather under him.

"Now you have your exchange, Death." I yelled inside my own head.

The heat and pressure eased slightly, as I felt Death move towards the injured shifter. Leonardo's body gave up and his son released his neck. I watched as his body stilled. I chanted over Fern faster and louder pulling on all my power. The fire sparked and crackled intensely sending out purple flecks of flame.

I laid my hands on Fern and commanded him to live. The atmosphere in the cave cooled to a bearable temperature and I knew that Death had taken Leonardo's spirit and gone.

Fern would heal and live. The large cat padded over to me and licked the wound on my wrist.

"Go ahead and mark me," I said. He hung his head and walked back to the limp body of his dead father.

To my surprise two more jaguars walked into the cave and padded toward me. One was sleek black and the other was much smaller and had a beautiful brown coat of fur with darker brown rosettes sprinkled over its body. The black jaguar nuzzled my head and neck, before walking over towards his brother. The two male jaguars were almost identical. They greeted each other with a low growl.

"Would either of you like to tell me what's going on?" I asked, no longer sure which jaguar was which brother.

"They are working together," Luciana purred. She was the beautiful brown jaguar. "Isn't it wonderful?"

"Yes, but …" I began to answer watching her dress in clothes from a bag that she had been carrying on her back.

"Mrs. Barnardos, what's going on?" Fern asked.

"Oh, Fern. Thank goodness you're okay." His eyes were open halfway. His lids looked heavy like he was fighting sleep. His breathing pattern was almost back to normal.

"I have a feeling I have you to thank for that," he said.

"That's not important. I'm just glad that you are going to be fine." I helped him sit up against the cave wall. His wound was almost completely healed. I handed him a bag of cookies from his backpack and a bottle of water. He would need to eat and rest a little longer before we could move him.

"Help me find clothes for them," I said to Luciana. I pointed to the duffle bag that was in the corner of the cave.

"Not necessary," she said coming closer to me. She opened her large leather pack. Inside the bag was enough clothes for all three jaguars to get dressed. She handed me one set of the men's clothing as she walked towards the jaguars who were pacing around their dead father's body.

Both jaguars phased into their human forms and dressed in the clothes that Luciana had carried. To my surprise it had not been Marco who defeated and killed his father, but Adriano. My head swiveled back and forth between the two handsome brothers.

"But, wait. I don't understand. What's …" I began to say.

"I know you thought I was Marco," Adriano interrupted. I nodded, noticing a nasty looking gash on his neck. His father must have bit him pretty deep during their fight. He lifted his hand to his neck and touched the wound. "I'm faster … remember," Adriano said, smiling proudly.

"Yeah, we know but I'm smarter," Marco chimed in, patting his brother on the back. "Smart enough to figure out a way to make you do the right thing for a change."

"Well, if you're so smart how come I'm the new CEO of Barnardos' Coffee," Adriano said, pulling the lovely Luciana in for a kiss.

I raised an eyebrow and looked at Marco. Apparently Marco gave his position in the company to his brother and found a way to get Luciana and Adriano back together.

"If he is the CEO then what does that make you?" I asked.

"I'm going to be busy opening my wife's new medical clinic," he said casually, like I was just supposed to know what he was talking about.

"I didn't realize you were engaged," I replied.

"Why don't we get the boy back to his house," Luciana

said to Adriano, who nodded at her cue to leave.

Marco and I watched as they helped Fern out of the cave with our camping supplies.

"Before we discuss engagement there is something we need to take care of," Marco said pointing to his father's dead body.

"What are we supposed to do with him?" Mr. Barnardos' body was still in the form of a jaguar. Marco explained that shifters maintain whichever form they were in when they die because both forms are natural to them.

"I'll have to burn his body," he said.

"You don't seem upset about his death," I commented.

"No, he was a horrible father and a worse human being."

The camp fire was still burning but it was not going to be big enough to burn the body of a large jaguar. We gathered broken branches and dead leaves into a pile then Marco arranged some of the larger branches over the pile creating a platform to place his father. He then carried the jaguar over to the funeral pyre and lit it with one of the branches from the camp fire.

We stood there watching his father's body burning. I turned to watch him and lifted my fingers to wipe the tears falling from his eyes. He did care about his father no matter what he said. He looked down at me grabbing my fingers and kissed the tips gently.

We walked back through the rainforest to the clearing where an off-road vehicle was parked waiting to take us back to the plantation.

Instead of driving back to his home, Marco kept on driving until we arrived at the beach. I didn't question him. I figured that he needed more quiet time.

We walked along the beach until we found a familiar spot. Several blue beach umbrellas were set out for rental along with a handful of larger cabanas that offered privacy.

Marco paid to rent one of the cabanas, selecting the one farthest away from the others. He lifted the gauzy white curtain and motioned me inside. We sat against the fluffy pillows looking out at the waves crashing against the sand. The light from the setting sun sparkled like diamonds across the crests of the waves. Marco lifted the hair from my neck and kissed the skin below my ear. I closed my eyes in reaction to the long awaited pleasure. A soft moan escaped my lips as his mouth explored my neck and shoulders.

"Marco," I whispered.

"Hmmm," he responded between kisses.

"Are you going to mark me?" I asked, the words coming out in breathy gasps between the spikes of pleasure rippling through me.

He stopped and looked me in the eye. I wondered what he was thinking. Then as one corner of his mouth curved in a slow smile, I knew. I knew that he knew what I was thinking. I wanted to be marked. I wanted to no longer wait this slow and torturous waiting. His mark would end all the years of hurt, rejection, pain, and longing. His mark would reaffirm his desire for me. I would be his forever and better yet he would be mine. For the other men, those lesser men, the mark had made me their possession, but for Marco the mark would make him equally mine. We would be each other's possession. Equals.

His mouth lowered back to my neck. I felt his tongue languishing on one spot toward the back of my neck. Then I felt his teeth change. They were bigger and sharper and before I could even feel any fear of pain, they were piercing my skin. I could feel the blood filling his mouth, as his tongue worked to close the wound, and stop the bleeding.

"You are mine now," he said moving to lay beside me and gliding his fingers over the small mark on my neck.

Suddenly my breath caught in my lungs, as a wave of emotions over took me –his emotions. His love, desire and complete happiness were swirling around with my own emotions inside my head. He was kissing me within seconds of the realization at we were sharing emotions. He could feel just how much I wanted him … only him. He was going to give me everything I wanted. His kiss promised me an end to my torment.

www.ingramcontent.com/pod-product-compliance
Lightning Source LLC
Chambersburg PA
CBHW060929120626
46557CB00003B/924